MADDIE MARZOLA

Skaara Signal

First published by Bonafide Publishing 2025

This novel is entirely a work of fiction. The names, characters and incidents portrayed in it are the work of the author's imagination. Any resemblance to actual persons, living or dead, events or localities is entirely coincidental.

Maddie Marzola asserts the moral right to be identified as the author of this work.

First edition

ISBN: 978-1-917686-02-0

This book was professionally typeset on Reedsy.
Find out more at reedsy.com

To my found Family.

Blowing warm breath in her cupped hands only worked so far. Lucy pushed her hands deep in her pockets, trying to preserve the heat for a few seconds longer.

She would have given anything for some warm spring sun, anything to break a winter that looked as if it was going to last forever.

"Open the door, would you?"

She looked up to see Matthew, tall and rugged, with his broad shoulders and chiselled features – the man who had become a safe harbour in the recent hurricane of events that was her life. The word *boyfriend* felt childish, as if they were still fifteen and walking home from school together, yet that was inevitably the only way to describe him.

He was walking up the pavement and towards her, carrying one of the few boxes that contained all of Lucy's possessions. It was almost sad to think that her whole life could fit in only one carload.

She pushed the front door of the three-storey house Matthew's parents owned in one of the wealthiest neighbourhoods in Bristol. To his family's standards, it still looked like a shack.

"Do you need a hand?" she asked.

"I'm good, thanks. If you get the last box, we're all done."

She glanced a few steps away to see Frank peeking from behind the box he was carrying. He walked right past her and through the open door. She barely had time to think of something to say before he disappeared inside.

She exhaled a white cloud of breath and walked over to the car. Her friend Sophie was still sitting in the driver seat, the engine on and the heating on full blast.

"Are you sure about this?" she asked when Lucy sat next to her in the passenger seat.

"I can't live on your sofa forever," replied Lucy.

Sophie shook her head. "It's a spare room for us, and you know what I mean."

Yes, Lucy knew what she meant. "It's the right thing to do."

"And since when you worry about doing the right thing?"

Sophie's sharp words stabbed deep at Lucy's open wound. A sharp inhale betrayed her pain, and realisation dawned on Sophie. It would have been a fair point only a few months back, but a lot had changed since then. "I'm sorry, I shouldn't have said that."

Her throat already tightening, Lucy battled the tears coming, as she murmured, "I told you. I'm not that person anymore."

Sophie shifted in her seat and turned to Lucy with a worried frown. "All you told me is that last November Matthew brought you and Frankie on a hike, that you found something in the woods, and that you and your brother got locked up for two weeks because of that. How does that connect to you moving in with him today, a full three months later?"

"It's not as simple as that."

"Because of the thing you found in the woods, I know. The one you can't talk about, and the same one that got your secret agent friend killed in some sort of superhero explosion."

She was missing a lot of classified details, but Sophie had the gist of it.

Three months earlier, a spaceship had landed in the Forest of Dean, and Lucy was part of the trio that found it, together with Matthew and her brother Frank. The pilot of the spaceship was a small, slithery alien of a species called Skaara, who turned out to be able to play puppet master to anything with a brain on it. Frank had a first-hand demonstration of it right away.

It was for Frank's sake that Lucy had accepted to help the Skaara that day, although that hadn't worked out well for anyone in the end. The secret agent friend – Agent Stephanie Davis of the mighty SafeOp Security Services – eventually had to swoop in and save the day, blowing up both Skaara and the spaceship, as well as herself. Big hero moment.

All of that because Lucy had chosen to help the Skaara.

"I'm responsible for what happened. I just think..." Lucy paused, her voice catching as a lump rose in her throat. She took a shaky breath while Sophie's hand was already on her shoulder, soft words telling her it was okay. It wasn't okay, though. With the next breath, Lucy continued, "I just think she'd still be alive if it wasn't for me. I screwed up, and I don't want to screw up anymore."

Her words lingered in the warmth of the car for a moment, accompanied only by her soft sniffling.

After a few breaths, Sophie gently said, "If moving in with Matt is what you feel is the right thing to do, then you have my full support, you know it. And you can always come back if this doesn't feel right anymore. You hear me?"

Lucy answered with a nod, then shook her head as she wiped the tears off her face – she had no idea how she felt. "For now, would you be able to support me with a tissue?"

"Of course." Sophie reached into the glove compartment and produced a pack of tissues.

A few moments later, when Lucy opened the car door to the freezing winter air, she liked to believe that no sign of her crying spell lingered on her face. She took the last of the boxes from the boot and waved at Sophie for the last time.

Matthew was waiting for her by the door.

He stopped her on the way through to plant a kiss on the corner of her lips. "Are you okay?" he asked as he pulled back.

She leaned into him, hoping he hadn't noticed she had been crying, and let his presence hold her up for a moment. "Yeah, it's just really cold," she said, sniffling still. "Where's Frankie gone?"

"He's upstairs. We thought hot chocolate would be a good idea. The café round the corner is supposed to be the best in the Southwest of England. I won't be a minute." He said it with a smile, and he probably meant it too.

"Be quick," she pleaded.

Matthew sighed. "He's your brother."

"Still. Be quick," she insisted. "And bring marshmallows. Lots of them."

As the door closed between them, Lucy made her way up the stairs to the first floor, which Matthew's parents had converted into a three-bedroom flat before kindly gifting it to their only son.

She leaned against the door, hoping it would give in to her weight. Unfortunately, closed doors hardly do that. With a disappointed grimace, Lucy put the box down on the floor so that she could knock and get her brother to let her in. As she leaned down, though, the box flaps came open, and something caught her eye.

There were things that Lucy had kept from Matthew in the weeks following the explosion, one of which was a small black box she had taken from Matthew's father – another of the things she had done for the Skaara. She didn't even know why she was asked to take it, nor what it was, yet her instincts were screaming at her to keep that to herself.

She grabbed the box, a small thing the size of a can of Coke, and dropped it in the biggest pocket of her winter jacket.

After knocking on the door, it was only a few moments before Frank opened the door. When he did, he lingered awkwardly, watching her go past. Neither of them said a word.

Compared to the outside world, Matthew's flat was a furnace. Lucy dropped the cardboard box next to the others in the living room, then hastily took off her jacket.

She turned to the coat hanger in the hall, then changed her mind halfway through the movement. She didn't want anyone accidentally noticing the alien parcel. Instead, she folded her jacket carefully and placed it over the boxes.

From the kitchen, she could hear Frank moving chairs and setting plates. She didn't know what he was doing, and she wasn't dying to ask him.

Once upon a time, she would've walked into the kitchen with a joke, something about her brother playing housemaid to her boyfriend or how he would've made such a better wife than she would. Once upon a time, he would have chuckled and thrown the dishrag at her.

Things had never been the same since the explosion. Frank couldn't remember any of that, she knew. He had been knocked out early in the day when the Skaara-controlled Edward Cook had shot him with a tranquilising gun. He had woken up later that evening in the back of a van, a headache the only unpleasant souvenir.

In the three months since then, they had been largely avoiding each other. Not a difficult task, considering Frank had spent Christmas with their parents as usual, while Lucy hadn't been on speaking terms with them since she was sixteen.

Despite that, Matthew was right. He was both her brother and Matthew's best friend. Lucy couldn't go on avoiding him forever.

She walked to the kitchen door and stopped on the threshold. Frank was emptying the dishwasher, carefully drying any glass that still showed any condensation.

"Are you interested in a position as maid of the house?" she joked tentatively.

He started and turned to her. "I thought you'd be unpacking your boxes."

Lucy's smirk turned sour. "I don't really know where to put any of that yet. I've got to wait for Matthew."

Frank's face dropped. "Oh. Right."

She watched him wring the dishcloth, pulling at the seams while his eyes searched the floor. Crossing her arms on her chest, she casually leaned against the door jamb with affected coolness. "Do you need a hand?" she offered.

A rattle of keys came from the front door before Frank could answer, and Matthew made his way through the front door. "Never fear, I come with chocolate!" he announced.

Lucy walked up to him with a smile of relief. "I'll take these," she said, grabbing the takeaway cups so he could take off his coat.

Back in the kitchen, Frank was leaning against the counter. The dishwasher was closed behind him. He looked as if he was going to say something. Before he could, however, Matthew was right next to her. "I asked for extra marshmallows for both of you. How's that for a housewarming gift?"

Frank shrugged and gave him half a smile. "Feels like Christmas."

Lucy looked closely at her brother's expression as he grabbed his hot chocolate. His face looked as if he was expecting it to be poisoned, yet had quietly accepted the inevitability of it. He then pulled a chair, sat at the table and wrapped his hands around the hot cup.

The mood hadn't escaped Matthew's attention either. "Hey, Frankie, cheer up! We're celebrating, remember?"

Frank beamed at Matthew in return. "Moving Day," he replied.

"Here's to my new home," said Lucy, raising her hot chocolate in a toast.

Matthew raised his takeaway cup with her. "How do you like your marshmallows?"

She opened the lid of her cup to look at the multitude of sugary lumps bobbing on the surface. "There's indeed a lot of them here," she conceded.

"To think we wouldn't be here if it wasn't for your mum," added Frank casually.

All eyes turned to him. Lucy was the first one to speak. "What do you mean by that exactly?"

"She's the one who sent us on that hike in the woods, re-member?" he explained, while his gaze remained trained on Matthew, who cleared his throat as if he was about to say something, only to get busy sipping his hot chocolate.

Lucy's memory returned to how Matthew's mother had come out of nowhere with a suggestion for a hike in the Forest of

Dean. She had never taken an interest in Matthew's life and activities, yet she had been very insistent on them going that very weekend.

"Matthew, any particular reason your mum told us to go on a hike that turned our life into an episode of X-Files?"

Matthew's eyes lingered on the hot chocolate in front of him, his thumb tracing slow, deliberate circles against the side of the cup. "Well, probably because she knew."

I can't have heard that right, she thought. As if her boyfriend's mother could know that a spaceship had landed. As if all the trials they had suffered since then had been somehow pre-ordained. That couldn't be possible. Lucy wasn't even sure how to absorb the information while Matthew sat silent, his eyes roaming the room like a child pretending innocence in front of a spilt carton of milk he had clearly knocked off.

"I beg your pardon. Did you say she knew about the space-ship?" she eventually asked.

"I know what you're thinking, but I didn't know either, at least not about the spaceship, and when they told me, after everything you both were going through, I didn't know how to bring it up, okay?" he rushed to say, leaning back on his chair as if expecting a blow.

The snap from Lucy, however, was only verbal. "So you waited for me to move in with you?"

Despite her sharp tone, it wasn't anger that Lucy was feeling. She thought she had moved into a place of safety, yet the first conversation was about betrayal. She was disappointed and a little more wary than she had been that morning. She wondered if Sophie had already arrived home and if it was too early to ask her to turn back.

Tapping her fingers nervously on the table, Lucy watched the marshmallows slowly sink into her hot chocolate.

After a couple of uncomfortable seconds too many, Matthew shifted nervously in his chair. "It was part of some project they've been working on. My parents knew that something from outer space was going to land somewhere in the UK," he started, and Lucy was sure she could spot a glint of pride in his eyes. "They thought it would land somewhere up north, but something went wrong, and it landed in the Forest of Dean instead, so they asked me to go pick it up."

He explained it as if Mr and Mrs Cavell had simply asked him to pick up some milk from the shop instead of retrieving an alien spaceship.

Sat directly in front of Lucy, Frank was staring down at the table. She might not have spoken a lot with her brother in the previous few months, but she could still read the lines on his face. "You knew," she murmured.

"I didn't, actually," he corrected her. "I figured it out later."

She turned her attention away from him before saying something she'd regret later. After all, he wasn't the one who had been lying to them since the beginning. "How did your parents know about a spaceship coming to Earth?"

That wasn't what she wanted to know, but it came close enough. Lucy thought of Agent Davis, and how she gave her life to stop the Skaara's plan to colonise the planet. Even Frank, in his absurd idea of a good plan, had risked everything to blow up the Skaara spaceship. Yet, Matthew's parents had known of the landing all along and had even sent them as an impromptu welcome party. The question she wanted to ask wasn't *how*, but *why*.

"I don't know how they knew, but I'm glad they did," replied Matthew. "You've seen what one can do. If a whole army comes down, I'd rather be prepared for it."

Lucy wished she could toss the whole load of marshmallows at him.

Frank stepped in to distract her from the thought. "How are they planning to prepare, exactly? It's a mind-controlling species with interplanetary travel technology. If they start a war, we won't stand a chance."

Matthew shrugged. "Well, if we learn enough about them, we'll have a better chance, don't you think? Knowledge is power, after all."

Lucy let her head drop in her hands. Matthew had no idea what he was talking about. He hadn't experienced what dealing with the Skaara looked like in practice. He hadn't seen Davis's face after a whole day of being under their control. He hadn't seen Edward Cook's vacant stare when Gwyn – the Skaara scout that landed with the spaceship - used a satellite part of her brain to remote control him like a toy robot. They had already almost lost a war against a single Skaara, and Matthew's attitude made her believe they should have.

Lucy closed her eyes and shook the memory away. Those events were in the past, and the past had to stay where it was.

"Well, that doesn't really matter anymore, does it?" she said, then took a large sip of her hot chocolate to mark the statement.

"I wouldn't be too sure about that," countered Matthew. "Wherever the first alien came from, there will be others."

"Luce is right, Matt," interjected Frank, and for once, Lucy was grateful. "Not that it doesn't matter at all, but it's none of our concern."

"Says the one who was concerned enough about this to bring explosives into a military base," replied Matthew.

Frank sighed heavily. "I thought we were past that."

Lucy had no patience to sit through that conversation anymore. "Whatever," she murmured, then pushed back her chair in a move to get up and walk out of the room. "The spaceship is gone, and the alien is dead. That's all I want to know."

Before she could even reach the door, however, Matthew's comment froze her in her tracks. "You might have to revisit that."

When she turned, Frank was staring at Matthew just as wide-eyed as she was. Lucy could guess by herself what he meant. "Gwyn survived."

Matthew shook his head. "You should really stop calling it that."

"That's her name," Lucy shot back. "She's alive, isn't she? What have you done with her?"

She feared the answer to the question. It was too easy to imagine what must have happened to Gwyn if she had been captured again.

"They didn't tell me," he said, then hesitated before adding, "Listen, I think you should help. Considering all you've been through and all you know about the Skaara. You and Frank both."

He glanced around the table in an attempt to gather consensus. Lucy could hardly believe he was even asking her that. "You must be joking," she said.

The look on Frank's face reflected the way she was feeling, with a frown on his face that alone questioned Matthew's sanity. "Help you with what?"

Matthew chuckled at Frank's question. "Don't make that face. There's nothing dangerous going on. Nobody is going to shoot rockets at the aliens or anything like that."

His cheerfulness made Lucy want to slap him across the face.

"Great, then better if we just stay out of the way and let your parents do their peaceful world-saving thing."

"Considering what happened last time you got involved, I agree. You should stay out of it."

Frank's words hit Lucy like a freight train. She felt the anger rising, and words came pouring out of her mouth before she could stop them. "That's rich coming from you. I should stay out of it, but you're free to jump back in? Is that what your therapist recommended for you to get closure?"

The only response she got was a deep sigh as Frank slumped against the back of his chair. Lucy had to battle the tears rising to her eyes and was thankful for once for Matthew's intervention.

"How about we start with something easy? Low commitment. Interactions strictly between humans," he offered, then turned to Lucy, a hand reached out across the table, inviting her to sit down with them again. "Luce, what do you say? Maybe it'll be good for the two of you to do something together. Maybe you could both find closure."

Lucy stared at his proffered hand.

That's bullshit, and no way to find closure, she thought. Under no circumstances was she going to sit back down at the table. "What's this low-commitment thing, exactly?" she asked.

Matthew smiled as if he had already won. "We're going to meet my uncle."

Lucy and Frank started in simultaneous shock. "You have an uncle?"

"My mother's brother," he explained. "They haven't been on speaking terms for a long time. Something to do with the woman he married, I think."

Lucy scoffed. "He married the gardener's daughter or something?"

"No, I don't think that was it," he mused, then shrugged. "That's not the point, though. He was the one who first found out the Skaara were about to land."

The more Matthew talked, the more Lucy's nerves tensed. She crossed her arms on her chest to hide her hands nervously clutching the air. It felt like a trap. As long as she stayed with him, Lucy felt like she was living in alien central.

Her ears were buzzing as her mind struggled, and her mind struggled to accept the inevitability of it all. As Frank and Matthew's conversation veered toward directional transmitters and radio signals, it sounded to her like nothing more than background noise.

Her mind drifted to Sophie once again. She could still move back in with her and leave Matthew and Frank to deal with the estranged uncle and the alien threat. All she had to do was send a text message. If only she could be sure that was the right thing to do.

She had been selfish before, and someone else had paid the price. She didn't want the same thing to happen to Frank, nor to Matthew.

As she tuned back into the conversation, Frank was saying, "You think they're going to send another spaceship?"

"It stands to reason," replied Matthew with the same matter-of-fact attitude he would have used to say that the sun would go down at sunset. "We destroyed the first one they sent, so it makes sense they'd want to retaliate."

"I thought you said no one will be battling an alien army." Even Lucy's sarcasm sounded dejected.

Matthew ignored her tone. "We're trying to avoid that."

"By imprisoning and experimenting on their ambassador?"

she retorted.

"That thing is hardly an ambassador," he replied, quickly closing the argument. He stood up, then, leaving his half-finished hot chocolate on the table. "I'll organise everything for the trip this weekend."

"Where are you going?" asked Lucy. She dreaded being left alone with Frank, especially after the conversation they had just had.

"I have a few phone calls to make," he replied dismissively. "Do you want to pick a film to watch later?"

He left a kiss on her cheek as he brushed past her, barely making eye contact. He was already out of the room when Lucy nodded and replied. "Sure."

Lucy felt herself waver. She reached out a hand to steady herself against the chair while the fast flow of events sent her adrift. Her thoughts returned to the black box she had hidden in the pocket of her jacket. Whatever it was, the Skaara asked her to steal it from Matthew's father. She had never stopped to consider how they had known it was there or how it got there to begin with. More than ever, she felt she had to keep it hidden, at least until she figured out what it was and who she could trust with it.

She wished Agent Davis were still alive. She would have known what to do with it.

Frank was still sitting at the table, sipping his hot chocolate and checking something on his phone. Seeing him like that reminded her of another piece of the puzzle she had left behind – another secret she had kept for herself.

"Do you still have the pink sloth?" she asked the silent room.

Frank was caught mid-sip. He quickly swallowed and looked up. "Um, yeah. I must have it at home somewhere."

Lucy nodded. "I just thought, maybe I could have it back? Call me nostalgic, but I feel like rewatching those videos you made for me."

That wasn't all of it. When she had freed the Skaara scout from the quarantined laboratory, she had managed to download the research material stored on the computer. At the time, she had considered it insurance in case something went wrong. When things did go wrong, however, she realised the last thing she needed was a flash drive full of stolen intel, so she had left it with Frank, the one person she could always rely on.

Or at least that's what she thought at the time.

"Oh, sure." He then shifted his gaze back to the screen of his phone, if only to lock it and put it away in his pocket. "I have an early day tomorrow, and still some stuff to do. I think I'll be off."

He didn't wait for a reply before heading to the front door, almost brushing Lucy's shoulder on his way to retrieve his coat. "Say bye to Matt for me, would you?"

It was clear he was just as eager to have some one-on-one time with her as she was. He was already out of the door when Lucy managed to reply. "Sure. See you later, Frankie."

A minute later, Lucy stood at the living room entrance, a tepid hot chocolate in her hands. Her winter jacket was still neatly folded on the cardboard box, just like she left it. Matthew's voice came muffled from down the hall: he was still on the phone in his office-converted spare room.

She took one last sip, then placed the cup on one of the boxes before unfolding her jacket. She brought the black box out of the pocket and unwrapped the newspaper covering it. As soon as the box came into view, though, she dropped it as if it were on fire.

It fell on the carpet with a soft thud, and Lucy instinctively stepped back.

The box was still there and still black, yet it was somewhat pulsing, as if a heart was beating inside it – a silent *tu-tum-tu-tum* of intermittent darkness.

Black became shinier, then darker, then shinier again.

Slowly, Lucy bent down to pick it up.

It felt neither warmer nor colder, neither heavier nor lighter.

As a chill ran down her spine, Lucy came to the realisation that what she was holding was much more than a simple box. In many ways, it felt like a death sentence.

- II -

There was a faint light coming through from behind the curtains. It must have been morning already.

Former Agent Stephanie Davis had lain on her bed for a few hours already, fully dressed, half asleep and half bracing herself for the day ahead.

She had woken up in that same room around three months earlier – what felt like a whole year to her – with three bruised ribs, a broken arm, and the feeling that it made no sense for her to still be alive. Since then, only a wall calendar in the kitchen had told her that Christmas had passed, and January had come and gone, leaving her in the middle of February, none the wiser to what had brought her there.

She vaguely remembered the events that led to the explosion, from the Skaara spaceship hidden in the hangar to Edward Cook, her boss and Chief of Operations for SafeOp Defence Services, who had lived his last few days as a mind-controlled tool of the Skaara alien they had had in custody.

The Skaara, on the other hand, she remembered very clearly. It had taken one wrong move, and the small, slithery alien settled behind her shoulders, taking full control of her body while she remained conscious and helpless spectator to the events.

17

Events had escalated when the Skaara had relinquished control. Stephanie had broken free and placed the explosives to destroy the spaceship, the pods it carried, and the alien with them.

The last thing she remembered was the Chief holding her at gunpoint. He hadn't fired. The explosion came first.

No matter how many times she went through the events, everything told her she should have died there.

Yet here I am, she thought. *Somebody up there must like me very much.*

Once she found out about the security team assigned to keep her in custody, however, it became clear that it wasn't by divine intervention that her life had been spared – and certainly not out of charity.

A self-proclaimed physiotherapist had cleared her for exercise shortly after her ribs had stopped aching That had marked the start of her walks on the grounds surrounding the house, testing the boundaries of her confinement. She soon found that these boundaries were closer than she expected and protected by fences on the northern and eastern sides, while a thick, high hedge surrounded the rest of the perimeter.

Escape, however, wasn't off the cards, as long as Stephanie gave herself time to heal. In the meantime, she had taken notes.

She stood up from the bed and opened the curtains. From the first-floor window, she could see the front yard and the garage opposite. The SUV was parked under the bare beech tree, as usual. The green Ford Fiesta, on the other hand, was a novelty.

Something had changed.

As she prepared to leave the room, she checked for her house keys and wallet, the only personal effects she had been allowed to keep. If she could get her hands on the key to the backdoor, that was all she needed to make her way out of there.

It wasn't the first attempt to leave that place, yet the pressure to succeed weighed heavily on her hand every time she reached the door handle. Stephanie took a deep breath, then opened the door and stepped out into the hall. All was quiet.

Making her way down the stairs and into the kitchen, she listened for any sign of life. The house wasn't usually that quiet in the morning. She moved around the kitchen table and towards the backdoor. The key should have been in the drawer closest to it. When she opened it, though, she could only see some pins and a pair of paper scissors.

"Agent Davis!"

That voice, like a ghost from a nightmare. It was all Stephanie could do not to throw the paper scissors as she turned around.

On the doorway, a round woman in a blue angora sweater was grinning at her. "I was wondering when you'd wake up! Come have a sit."

Victoria Evans had been administration support at SafeOp before the spaceship explosion caused the security agency to go bust. She had made herself a reputation for being the most enthusiastic non-operative person on the floor. There had been some teasing about it, but people mostly found her endearing.

Except for Stephanie. She had never liked Victoria very much. After three months of talking to nobody but unresponsive security agents, she still wasn't ready to revisit that feeling. Even so, Victoria was a source of information she couldn't overlook. Stephanie gritted her teeth and did her best to smile. "Victoria. What are you doing here?" she asked, surreptitiously placing the scissors back in the drawer and closing it behind her, wondering if Victoria had seen any of that.

Only then did Stephanie take the time to look at the woman

carefully. Her smile looked forced, and her skin looked pale, with dark circles around her eyes. Life couldn't have been too kind to her since they last met.

In one excited breath, as if trying to deny her appearance, Victoria explained, "Why, I heard you were getting better and stronger, and I thought I'd come and see for myself before you make a run for the hills! It looks like I got here just in time."

"I'm here. You saw me. Mission accomplished. Well done," replied Stephanie, giving Victoria a half-hearted thumbs-up.

"Indeed! Glad I could catch you before your breakaway. Let's have a chat."

As Victoria took a seat at the table, Stephanie considered the options. "Can I grab a coffee first?"

Victoria gestured to the kitchen counter behind her. "Be my guest."

The coffee machine was in the corner of the countertop. Stephanie picked one of the coffee pods and dropped it in the machine, then pressed the green button to start it. A whirring noise filled the silence for a few precious seconds while Stephanie gathered her thoughts.

As soon as silence was restored, Victoria rushed to break it again. "You know, it's actually funny to say that. This is my house! You already are my guest!"

Stephanie stopped mid-turn, processing the new information before walking back to the table and taking a seat opposite the newly discovered owner of the premises.

"Oh, I know what you're thinking," the woman continued. "If it's my house, why haven't you seen me here before, right? Well, I wouldn't live here on my own in the middle of nowhere!"

"Why are you here now, then?" asked Stephanie.

"As I said, you and I need to have a chat!"

Stephanie nodded. Information was what she needed, and Victoria was offering it willingly. Even so, there was little chance Stephanie could withstand a whole conversation with a pretend-jolly Victoria Evans without punching the exclamation marks out of her mouth – together with her teeth, likely. She could generally hold her nerves, but Victoria was overdoing it.

She took a tentative sip of her coffee, hoping the brew would help her cope. It was still very hot, but the gesture alone seemed to help. "Are you going to tell me how I got here and what you want from me?"

Victoria nodded. "All of that, yes. First, there's something else you need to know." She gripped the coffee mug and straightened her back, maintaining an unsettling eye contact. "You are dead."

Stephanie waited for the punchline.

"Not literally dead, of course! However, your bank account is frozen, your apartment has been repossessed, and your phone has been disabled. All the usual," she explained. "You see, to the world, you died in the explosion that took out Edward Cook."

It was a lot to process.

"The Chief is dead." Stephanie had expected as much, yet the news still jabbed at her stomach.

"Quite so, yes." Victoria dismissed the fact with a wave of the hand and moved on. "Now to more important things. A few years ago, you were stationed in South America, were you not?"

Not what Stephanie was expecting and certainly not something she cared to talk about. "No spaceships there," she replied, ice clinging on every word.

"Oh, of course not! It's quite established that the one you blew up was the first one that landed. Anyhow, as I was saying, South

America. You were still a rookie for SafeOp Defence Services at the time, weren't you? Cook's pet project. He paired you with one of the most experienced agents so you could learn from the best!"

It was suddenly clear where that was going. "Connor Evans," said Stephanie, her gaze wandering to the top of the table as she connected the dots between him and Victoria Evans. "He was your husband, wasn't he?"

She remembered him well, and she remembered how he died, leaving a widow to receive his casket when it landed back in England. Stephanie couldn't believe she had never made the connection. When she glanced at Victoria again, it was with different eyes – her constant enthusiasm turned into a thin veneer to hide the hurt she must have been carrying inside.

Victoria merely nodded. "There was another agent in the field with you, Oliver Bennett."

Stephanie remembered him too. "He went by his middle name, Damien. Fitted him better, if you ask me." She exhaled as she lowered her eyes, pausing to recall the events. "There was an organisation MI6 had identified as an exporter of bioweapons to Western Europe. One of those operations where they didn't want to send British agents overseas, so they asked SafeOp to take over. Damien was our contact in the organisation. We thought we could trust him."

"At the time, I didn't get it," resumed Victoria. "I got mad at SafeOp. I got mad at you, because you survived, while Connor didn't."

"I almost didn't either," interjected Stephanie. She had been lucky – luckier than she had deserved.

In the short time they had spent together, Damien had charmed her, almost converted her to the organisation's cause

– a terrorist motif disguised as the honourable mission of saving humanity from themselves.

By the time Stephanie had figured out what was really going on, Connor was dead, and she was facing the barrel of Damien's gun.

It was pure luck that the bullet hadn't killed her. Pure luck that she managed to find help in time.

"Anyway!" Victoria's burst shook Stephanie out of her reverie. "I'm not here to reminisce on sad stories. After the explosion at the landing site, SafeOp was dissolved. A lot of people went their own way, but Millican offered me a job. I took it, of course. Don't you want to get back out there too?"

Stephanie raised an eyebrow at the absurdity of that statement. "Millican as in the Director and CEO of SafeOp Defence Services Robert Millican?"

"The very same!"

"Is this a job interview?"

Victoria's face, a second before beaming with pride, suddenly turned to ice, the dark half-moons under her eyes growing darker. "You're not going to help."

"I don't know," replied Stephanie. "What am I helping with, exactly?"

Her enthusiasm restored, Victoria leaned forwards, hands gripping the table in excitement. "It's called Avis Carmen. Cool name, right?"

For a cult, yes, thought Stephanie. "It sounds ominous. What does it mean?"

"Oh, don't be silly now!" said Victoria, dismissing the question with a wave. "It's only in Latin to make it fancy. I believe it has something to do with birds and songs and whatever else. Not like there's an apocalypse in the making or anything like that."

Even Victoria didn't sound convinced by her own statement. Maybe the explanation wasn't entirely accurate, or maybe this Avis Carmen was really planning a Skaara genocide.

Only one way to find out, she decided, wondering how long it would take for her to regret her decision. "Okay," she conceded. "What sort of non-apocalyptic stuff are they planning, then?"

"Mostly research, while some of us help with the alien invasion side of things."

Victoria was doing that on purpose, throwing half-sentences and never offering any real explanation, keeping her interest alive and drawing her in. Stephanie recognised the technique and knew how to counter it. She sat back on her chair and silently waited.

Eventually, the silence became too much for Victoria to bear. "Of course, you probably figured that out already! With the little Skaara here on Earth and the spaceship blown to bits, it's only a matter of time before the rest of the aliens come charging with the big guns! It's obvious what needs to be done, really! The Avis Carmen operation is there to make sure that, when the aliens land again, they are given no chance for retaliation."

It sounded like a propaganda statement. It scared Stephanie to think how much of it Victoria truly believed. The silver lining to that nightmare manifesto, though, was the dazzling amount of intel it disclosed.

Gwyn was still alive, for starters. Back in a cage, for sure, but alive.

As for preventing retaliation, Stephanie doubted Avis Carmen could stop an army of Skaara should they decide to attack. With little hope for a positive response, she asked, "When you say they'll have no chance for retaliation, what do you mean? What are the countermeasures? Is the army involved?"

Victoria cackled as she waved another question away. "Oh no, Avis Carmen has better people for that purpose." She shook her head. Twice she seemed about to speak again, and twice she thought better of it.

Stephanie didn't rush her. The picture was coming together, and she took that pause in the conversation to consider the pieces of information she already had.

Hearing Millican's name had brought to mind the last mission she had been assigned to before Gwyn entered her life. Edward Cook, Chief of Operations, had sent her to the Scottish Highlands to investigate a radio signal of unknown origin. He had asked not to share the details of the case with anyone, especially Director Millican.

The investigation had been fruitless. The signal originated just outside the property of the Partridge family, recently married into Cavell.

There had been no evidence to link the Partridge family to a mysterious radio signal. At the time, the same was true about the Cavells, until their son casually stumbled onto a spaceship in the middle of the woods.

At the time, she hadn't made the connection. Matthew Cavell had sensibly stayed away from the spaceship and avoided an irritating month of quarantine, no doubt with some help from his parents' influence.

With the spaceship blown to pieces, SafeOp out of the picture and a new contingent of Skaara potentially on the way, who was there to recruit pawns for the self-elected saviours of the world if not Director Millican himself, the man who mustn't be informed of the operation to trace radio signal at the Partridge Estate.

Now, what are the odds, mused Stephanie between herself.

It was all conjectures at that stage, but Stephanie didn't have much to lose in making assumptions. "It's the Cavell family, isn't it? They are leading the Avis Carmen operation."

Victoria pointed an exultant finger at her. "See! I knew you were clever!"

Stephanie chose to ignore the implication that someone had told her she wasn't. "I was in the Highlands before the spaceship showed up in Herefordshire," she said, weighing her words. "I was tracing a signal coming from the Partridge Estate. That's Mr Cavell's wife, right?"

"It could be. I know that Mr Cavell's wife goes by Lady Partridge, but I don't know where all her summer residences are," offered Victoria, her expression betraying how little she understood the connection. "Anyway, that's all I came here to say! With the little Skaara not cooperating, I thought, who better to help than someone who's had first-hand experience with it?"

A chill ran down Stephanie's spine. "I'm not linking up with that thing again."

"Well, it's either you or the Campbells, so we'll have to figure something out. I'll be off now."

With that last comment, Victoria stood up from the table and headed towards the door, placing a heavy hand on Stephanie's shoulder on her way out. "Toodle-loo, my dear!"

It wasn't clear to Stephanie what was most uncomfortable: the heavy hand on the shoulder, the cheerfully ominous good-bye, or the blatant threat to the Campbells' safety.

This is bait. It must be bait. Lucy Campbell and her brother are clever enough to stay away from all this. Aren't they?

Whatever the case, Stephanie had to do something about it.

If an alien invasion was the worst-case scenario, a self-proclaimed protector of humanity that called itself *Avis Carmen* was a very close second.

She had to get out of there.

***

It was a cold night, and heavy clouds covered the waning moon. From her bedroom window, Stephanie had watched one SUV be replaced by another carrying the three security agents who were going to be stationed at the house that night.

Every exit was likely guarded, and every move outside her bedroom would invite suspicion. Even so, Stephanie couldn't wait for a better moment.

Making her way down the hall, she knew where the floorboards would creak, and she carefully chose her steps around them, sidestepping the corner of the carpet and brushing against the vase in the corner of the hall. As she took the stairs, she leaned against the bannister to skip two creaking steps. Once on the ground floor, the kitchen was only a few metres away. When she finally stepped through the doorway, she found it deserted.

It wasn't just the kitchen, though. The house was unexpectedly quiet. Wherever the three security guards had stationed themselves, they were being surprisingly inconspicuous. Unusual, yet not inconvenient. Stephanie reached for the drawer and found the key exactly where it was supposed to be – exactly where it hadn't been that morning.

It's a setup.

She knew it, just like she knew that Millican hadn't casually offered Victoria a job out of the kindness of his heart.

Stephanie slowly turned the key to open the door. The sound of the lock releasing was as loud as thunder in the darkness of the night. She paused to listen for anything that might hint at security coming to get her.

The house remained silent. The coast was clear.

As she carefully turned the door handle, though, she had to rethink her assessment.

"Who's there?" came a threatening voice from the kitchen door just as a flashlight shined in Stephanie's eyes, momentarily blinding her.

She didn't need to see to go on with her escape, anyway. She closed her eyes and opened the door, then slid behind it as quickly as she could, fully expecting the guard to shoot her with a tranquilising gun – the kind they had perfected to counter the Skaara, ironically – however, the shot never came.

There was no time to ponder on that, though, as the freezing February air hit her skin with a punch and filled her lungs. As she sprinted to the right, in the faint outdoor lighting, Stephanie eyed the hanging couch and the rowan tree to its side. She paused in the shadow of the garden furniture.

All three security agents should have been alerted by then, yet nobody seemed overly interested in her escape. Even the one that caught her in the kitchen had yet to pop his head out in the cold.

Nevertheless, Stephanie wasn't about to take any chances.

Coasting the side of the house, she reached the front yard and eyed the SUV parked under the tree. A moment later, she was crouching by the side of it, taking in her surroundings.

It was only then that the security detail showed up to their task, jogging out of the front door as if they were on a routine exercise. Stephanie listened to their measured steps while staying hidden behind the bulky vehicle.

The front gate was only a few yards away, locked. The only way out she could identify was the hedge on the western side. It was a longer run, but she knew she could make it – especially if security kept their vow of no shooting.

As the first of the guards reached the SUV, Stephanie darted towards the property's border, scanning for the best spot to cross, then dove past the hedge, frozen branches scraping at her face and clothes, until she emerged in the open countryside.

She stumbled to a stand with no time to catch her breath. She knew the road was somewhere to her right, coasted on the other side by a small patch of wood. Just what she needed.

She crossed the road and continued as deep as she dared amongst the trees. She kept on going, doing her best to keep the road in sight, and even when the trees weren't giving her cover anymore, Stephanie kept on running through the open field, with the moon still hiding behind the clouds and the stars shining light on her way forward.

She felt her breath burning in her chest and adrenaline pushing her muscles way past what she thought she could endure. She ran for what felt like hours, until the silhouette of a neighbouring house appeared past the trees. She slowed down to a walk just then, her heavy breath condensing in the night air.

It was not yet time to rest, though. Nobody seemed to be in pursuit, yet she couldn't be sure what game Victoria was playing. Maybe the SUV was following her at a distance.

The icy cold seeped through her thin jacket, urging her to move. Stephanie went on walking, feeling her bones trembling in her skin, until a spot of light in the distance caught her attention: a crossing, with its host of traffic lights and road signs.

If she could just keep on walking, she'd be back in Bristol before daylight, at which point she would start playing a game of her own.

It was a long road to Macclesfield, where Matthew's uncle had taken refuge after being shunned by the Partridge family.

Annoyed by an early start from Bristol, Lucy had demanded a stop at the first service station to gather breakfast. Frank had shrugged before settling in the backseat and promptly falling asleep. Matthew had been harder to convince but had eventually conceded when threatened by the prospect of having a sulking Lucy as his only conscious travel company.

As she returned to the car carrying her cheese-and-bacon toastie and black coffee, she couldn't help remembering the last time she had been at a service station with Matthew. It was the day of the explosion, and she had just lied through her teeth to convince Matthew to drive her all the way to the Wye Valley to help the Skaara in her quest. They had stopped for a reconciliatory bacon bap that time.

The journey to visit Matthew's uncle, however, felt a lot different.

As she headed back to the car, she could spot Frank's head against the back window, probably still dozing. Matthew, on the other hand, was pacing around, deep in conversation on his phone. With his back turned, he didn't notice Lucy.

"I know how important it is," he was saying, one hand

running through his hair while his face turned to the sky in annoyance. "Damien, he's my uncle. I'm sure I can..." he trailed off as he turned around to spot Lucy approaching. "Gotta go now. I'll call you when it's done."

"I didn't mean to interrupt. Is everything okay?" she asked.

"It was nothing," he said, dismissing it all with a wave. His frown, however, was telling a different story. "Did you get your coffee?"

Lucy raised her cup to show evidence of her successful journey to the service area. "Who's Damien?" she asked.

Matthew ignored the question and walked back to the car, leaving Lucy no choice but to drop the topic and follow.

* * *

It was already lunchtime when Matthew turned into the driveway of a small semi-detached house on the outskirts of Macclesfield. It reminded Lucy of her parents' house, with its blue door and brick-layered façade. For only a moment, she wondered about sharing that thought with her brother, but he was still dozing in the backseat – or at least pretending to do so.

As the car stopped, Lucy's stomach growled in response. The cheese-and-bacon toastie she had bought at the service station had only made her hungrier. She wondered what the chances were of Matthew's uncle offering tea and biscuits.

Matthew stepped out of the car as soon as the engine was off. Frank stumbled out, displaying his best impression of a waking beauty. Lucy opened the door and stepped on the driveway, then lingered there a bit longer, enough to see a fair-bearded man peer through the curtain of the living room window. The famed Uncle Jim, most certainly.

When she finally closed the car door and joined the boys at the door, Matthew was about to knock. Seconds later, the door opened on a tall and robust middle-aged man with a white mane of hair all around his face. It was an oddly satisfying appearance for the friendly neighbourhood alien hunter.

"I don't know you," he said as a way of greeting his visitors.

"Uncle Jim," said Matthew, spreading his arms as if expecting a hug, a sudden cheerfulness in his voice. "It's Little Mattie. Don't you remember me?"

The man's face wrinkled into a frown. He stepped back and away from his nephew's attempt at affection. "You're not so little anymore. Does your mother know you're here?"

"Not everything I do is because my mother tells me to. Besides, isn't it time you and my mum bury the hatchet?" His arms still open wide, he wasn't giving up on the hugging idea.

"Except when Lizzy buries one hatchet, she has five more in the cupboard ready to be thrown at you," was the sharp reply from the uncle.

Matthew shrugged as he lowered his proffered arms, pretending he didn't care his reconciliation gesture had been rejected. Lucy knew that wasn't the case. She felt she should have resented Uncle Jim for treating Matthew that way. Instead, she found herself liking him a little more. It was a relief to see he wasn't taking Matthew's friendliness at face value.

After careful consideration, Jim moved aside to let them all in, monitoring their steps as they entered the house.

"Mum always said you were the funny one," said Matthew on the way through, a fake joviality in his tone that Lucy had never heard before. She didn't understand what he was pretending to be. The whole thing was becoming unsettling.

Uncle Jim closed the front door and directed them to the living room. "Your mother never said such a thing, and I'd be grateful if you could drop the act."

Matthew didn't seem to pick up on the hostility of the remark as they walked into a cream-coloured room, where even the furniture looked sugar-coated. Jim's words were a zesty variation in that mellow climate.

Lucy followed Frank to the sofa after a brisk wave of their host.

"Fortunately, we're not here to talk about my mother," stated Matthew, as he sat on the only armchair, leaving Uncle Jim to be the last man standing in the room.

"What then? Do you want me to join your very own pyramid scheme?"

A smirk appeared on Matthew's face. His composure was almost disturbing. "Lucy and Frank were the first humans to have contact with the Skaara on Earth. I thought you might want to meet them."

The silence that followed was as thick as the cream that coloured the room. It felt to Lucy as if they had been chosen as bait for Uncle Jim's trap. She turned to Frank, expecting to see him as surprised as she was. He wasn't, though. He sat on the edge of the sofa, his hands on his knees, almost ready to spring. Lucy could picture his science brain gearing up for a Q&A session with the man who discovered the first alien species – and who could be instrumental in killing it off for good.

It didn't get any better when Frank spoke. "It's an honour to meet you, Mr Partridge," he said. "I hear you were the first to contact the Skaara that many years ago. Is it true you set up the communication system yourself?"

Lucy forgot how to breathe after hearing that.

The only person matching her shock seemed to be the estranged uncle. He was shifting his gaze intermittently from Lucy to Frank, as if that way he could judge what kind of scheme they were setting up. When he spoke, his tone was spookily subdued. "I forgot my manners. Would any of you like to help me in the kitchen with some tea and biscuits?"

He was looking at Frank and Lucy, clearly excluding Matthew from the selection. Frank didn't let him ask twice. "I'll help."

"That's not necessary," interjected Matthew, standing up to volunteer himself. "I can help Uncle Jim."

Frank, however, wasn't going to be deterred. "Don't be ridiculous, sit back down."

It was a ridiculous display, like watching two children arguing over who should be the next on the swing. Lucy wasn't going to be part of that. She stood up and walked out of the room, casting a meaningful glance at Uncle Jim, who quickly followed.

She heard Matthew calling her back to the living room and ignored him.

"Sounds like Mattie's mother hasn't hypnotised everyone just yet," commented Jim as they walked into the small kitchen down the hall.

Lucy turned those words around in her head. *Hypnotised* was maybe a strong word, yet it felt adequate to describe both Matthew's and Frank's behaviour. Maybe she was being paranoid, or maybe she had escaped hypnosis and was seeing things for what they were.

"Would you turn on the kettle?" he said, walking to the far end of the kitchen, as far away from the door as he could get.

"Is it true your sister isn't speaking to you because you married the gardener's daughter?" asked Lucy as she filled up the kettle.

The response came with a gentle chuckle. "At least Mattie

found someone funny to tag along with him."

Lucy frowned at him in disappointment. Jim's demeanour had changed since the mention of the Skaara, and Lucy feared he might be more inclined to help Matthew and his family's business than she had thought at first.

"That doesn't answer the question," she commented. She was still holding the full kettle in her hands.

He kept eye contact and gestured towards the kettle, inviting her once again to turn it on. "Please."

Unconvinced, she flipped the kettle switch. In a few seconds, the room filled with the noise of water slowly rising to boiling temperature. Only then did Uncle Jim start talking, a sense of urgency in his voice. "Is it true you were the one who found the Skaara?"

Finally, Lucy understood what was going on. "Yes, with Matthew and my brother. Frankie and I were the ones who approached the spaceship and met the Skaara face-to-face. Now you, is it true you were the first to talk to them?"

"Kind of," he replied quickly. "I stumbled on a Skaara capsule a few years back. It had instructions on how to communicate with their mothership. They don't really talk, but I suppose you can say that."

"Is that why you were kicked out of the family?" she asked.

He shook his head. "My sister was more than happy for my discovery."

"Why then?" insisted Lucy.

The kettle was close to boiling. Uncle Jim spoke fast. "My sister is not talking to me because I didn't want to move war on an unknown alien species."

The kettle clicked, and the noise subsided.

Lucy and Jim were staring at each other as if locked in some sort of duel. Eventually, it was Uncle Jim who broke eye contact, while a condescending smirk appeared on his face. "You're smarter than you look. You should use that."

He then turned to take four mugs from the cupboard. "The Skaara you met, it must have been one of their scouts. Would you happen to know where it is now? I wouldn't mind meeting it."

"It's a *she*, not a *it*," said Lucy before she could stop herself.

Jim shook his head. "Not true. Skaara are asexual beings. It's one of the first things I figured out when I tried to explain to them that I was a human male."

"Gwyn thinks of herself as *she*. I reckon they figured out the concept all right."

Jim chuckled at that remark. "Well said. Now, would you fill the mugs, and I'll get the biscuits."

As Lucy slowly poured water into each mug, Uncle Jim reached into one of the cupboards to produce a pack of biscuits before saying, "I can imagine what my sister is up to. She'll likely try to down one of their ships, strip it for parts, and use what she finds to create a monopoly on the technology. It's a clever plan. She's a very clever woman."

"Is that why you left? Because you didn't agree with her?" asked Lucy.

Uncle Jim, however, had gone silent. He was about to add a tea bag to each mug, when Lucy went to the sink and turned on the tap, then she quietly said, "There's something else. I took something from Matthew's father."

Uncle Jim suppressed a smile as he moved closer to the sink to allow for whispering. "Go on."

"It's a black box, except I don't think it's a box. It's black, and it kind of pulsates. Do you know what it might be?"

There was no mistaking the surprise on Uncle Jim's face. "You stole the beacon?"

"The what?" asked Lucy.

Matthew's voice, however, came from the hall before Uncle Jim could explain. "You two okay in there?"

Uncle Jim promptly called out, "We're all good. Be there in a minute."

As Matthew appeared at the door, Lucy turned off the tap.

"Lucy," he said, eyeing her suspiciously, "why don't you go back to join Frankie. I'll finish helping Uncle Jim here."

Lucy glanced at Jim for a moment. It was too soon. She needed more time with him to understand what that beacon was and what Matthew was trying to get her into.

Uncle Jim, however, seemed to be accepting the interruption quite peacefully. "I appreciate the help," he said amiably.

Lucy made her way out of the kitchen, then lingered in the hall as soon as she was out of sight, long enough to hear Matthew say, "We need to open a communication channel with the Skaara, and you're the only person who knows how to do that."

Uncle Jim's response was unwavering. "It's a hard pass, lad. I left my radio days behind me."

"Uncle Jim, they're sending another ship," insisted Matthew. "They're going to invade if you don't help us talk to them."

"You'll have plenty of chances when they touch down on Earth, don't you think? I'm sure you can figure something out. Now get me that tray over there. They'll be wondering what happened to their tea."

Just as Lucy was moving to get out of the way before getting caught, Frank popped his head from the living room. "Oh, you're there," he commented. "Is the tea ready?"

She headed back to join him in the living room and sat in

the armchair. "You can stand down, soldier," she mocked him. "We misjudged the kettle and had to boil it again," she explained, repeating Jim's excuse.

Frank scoffed but said nothing. He dropped back on the sofa and sat with his arms crossed on his chest, wearing the expression of someone who was thinking hard about something.

As for Lucy, she strained her ears to catch what was happening in the kitchen. However, their voices didn't carry that far.

Eventually, Matthew reappeared. He was alone. "Time to go," he said.

That could mean nothing good. "What do you mean? What about tea?" asked Lucy, glancing down the empty hall, worried Uncle Jim didn't seem to be on the way over to wave them goodbye, let alone give them tea.

Matthew dismissed her concern. "We'll get lunch on the way home."

Lucy stood dumbfounded. "Matthew, where's your uncle? What happened?"

He stopped and turned to look at her, a frown on his face as if he couldn't understand what was upsetting her. "He joined the cause," he said with a shrug. "Mission accomplished."

Lucy watched him stroll out of the front door. She wanted to go check on Uncle Jim, but her gut told her that would have only made things worse.

Meanwhile, Frank was already following Matthew to the car. He exhaled heavily as he pushed past her. "That was a long time to wait for no tea at all."

- IV -

From across the road, Stephanie watched the place that used to be her home. The window on the first floor pinpointed her living room – not that she could see any of the rooms from where she was. She couldn't even be sure her things were still there or that her key would still work.

After spending the night dozing off by the check-in desks at Bristol Airport, she took a bus back to the city, where she would look for a safe place to establish her base of operations. However, there was something else she had to take care of first.

The midday sun shining on her, she knew anyone could be watching her moves. She had to act quickly.

She crossed the road and took out her keys.

Mrs Widdicombe, the building administrator and downstairs neighbour, was likely listening to anyone coming in, ready to intercept them in the hall and share her latest grievances, as it was her habit. Stephanie wasn't looking forward to that.

The key slit into the keyhole and turned. The door opened, and Stephanie exhaled in relief. After retrieving the key, she let the spring mechanism close the door for itself with a loud clang as she darted up the stairs. She made it to the second landing before Mrs Widdicombe's croaky voice yelled out at her. "You couldn't hold that door and close it gently, could you? We'll all pay for it when it falls off its hinges!"

Ever dramatic, thought Stephanie. There was a part of her that missed having to suffer her ranting. It was easier than going into hiding while trying to prevent an alien invasion – or an interplanetary war.

The door of Stephanie's apartment was closed and locked, just like she had left it the morning of the explosion. She tried her keys, and sure enough, the lock turned and opened.

The space inside looked mostly untouched. When Victoria mentioned it being repossessed, she must have meant the Cavell family and their Avis Carmen operation. Not a reassuring thought.

Whoever had searched the place after her presumed death had done a good job at leaving things where she had left them, making it impossible for Stephanie to figure out what they may or may not have found in the process.

The only exception was her phone, which had disappeared from the coffee table, where the Skaara had forced her to leave it.

With no time to dawdle, she went to her bedroom to find her duffle bag and tucked in it as many shirts and underwear as she could find. Once that was done, it was back to the kitchen. From the cupboard, she took all the non-expired food she found and added it to the loot, together with her iron tablet – she had been fine without them for a short while, yet it wouldn't have been wise to overlook them, she decided.

Finally, she went to the sofa and pushed it as far towards the wall as she could without overbearing the recently mended bones of her left arm – enough to clear the carpet underneath.

She lifted the corner to reveal a hidden compartment where her metal safe was still securely concealed. Inside was her personal emergency package, including a gun, spare cash, a couple of fake passports, spare keys to every door in the building, and a set of keys to a semi-detached house near Montpelier Station. She hadn't been to that house in years, not since she had stopped sharing it with Roxy, her former partner.

Stephanie hesitated at the memory. Roxy had been on an undercover mission for two years after their breakup, which meant they hadn't spoken since. There was a risk she had been called back after SafeOp's dissolution and recruited into the Avis Carmen operation.

Roxy wouldn't buy into that, thought Stephanie.

Whatever the chances, it was a risk she had to take.

Stephanie dropped everything in the duffle bag and closed it.

Before making her way out, she took off her light jacket and threw it on the sofa, replacing it with her winter one. As she did that, something caught her eye. The device wasn't bigger than a fingernail, nested just above the seam behind the shoulder of the jacket, barely noticeable against the black fake leather. It was the exact spot where Victoria had touched her before leaving after their chat.

A tracker.

Of course they had been tracking her. That explained why it had been so easy to get away from them.

Stephanie wasn't sure what she was going to do with it. Still, she took it off the jacket, dropped it in her pocket, and made for the door.

Out of the apartment, she hadn't even made it to the stairs when she heard people talking on the ground floor. One of the voices she recognised as Mrs Widdicombe's.

"I did just like you said," she was explaining. "She went up the stairs, thought I didn't see her. Well, I tell you, I might be old, but I don't miss much."

Stephanie had heard enough. She took the bunch of keys out of the duffel bag and headed straight to the lower landing and the apartment one floor below. She silently opened the door, then disappeared inside just as two pairs of boots started up the staircase.

"Should we kick down the door?" a man said on her way up.

Victoria's snarky tone intervened to prevent undue damage to the property. "It's not always necessary to smash things down, Trevor."

Mrs Widdicombe, from the ground floor, hadn't missed the exchange. "What are you two confabulating up there? I'm gone one second to get the keys, and you already think of tearing down the whole place! I say, I almost wish I hadn't called you at all!"

Intent as she was listening to the events happening downstairs, Stephanie jumped at hearing a bellowing voice behind her. "Steph?"

Bob Colton, her dear friend and neighbour, charmingly nicknamed Beary Bob after the thick mane of hair covering his head and face. He had appeared down the hall and found her leaning against the door.

"Hey Bob," she whispered, slowly moving towards him. "I'm sorry to drop in like this after so long, buddy. How are you?"

"Okay," he said, a wary look on his face. "What are you doing here?"

Stephanie opened her mouth but failed to find the right words to explain herself. Eventually, she settled for the extremely short version. "I ran in some trouble, Bob. I need your help."

Lovely, kind-hearted Bob looked at her with a raised eyebrow and a trusting gaze. "Is it Mrs Widdicombe? She's been telling me off about the recycling again."

"It's not the recycling," she said, then paused, weighing the words to follow. "Mrs Widdicombe has some guests that are looking for me, and I can't let them see me."

Bob stood still for a moment. "Why are they looking for you?"

It was a fair question, Stephanie had to admit. "Bob, you know what I do for a living, right?"

Indeed, he was one of the very few who knew. "You're like James Bond, but you're real."

"And you know sometimes the bad guys go after James Bond, and he needs to sneak out of places without getting caught," she continued.

He nodded again. "Are those people here to kill you?"

There was a moment of hesitation. It wasn't that Stephanie didn't want to tell him. She just didn't know. "Could you help me sneak out from your window, please?" she asked instead.

Bob's eyebrow turned into a frown. "Steph, why were you weird last time you came here?"

Stephanie's heart sank. The last time they had met, the Skaara had been in control of her. She had been polite enough, yet she had also treated him like a stranger, which must have been very destabilising for Bob, someone who had become like a brother to her and who treated her like a sister.

"I wish I could explain, Bob," she said, reaching out to lightly touch his arm as if asking for permission to be his friend again, hoping he'd understand, forgive, and trust her again. He glanced down at her hand, then back at her face, but remained silent. She continued, "It wasn't me. I wasn't me. And I'm really sorry that I upset you."

To Stephanie's surprise, he smiled widely at that. "I knew that."

She smiled back, her chest filling with relief.

As if remembering the point of their conversation, Bob finally nodded. "It's too high to jump, Steph."

He was talking about the window. "I'm not going to jump. There's a drainpipe I can use. You'll see."

"You're too heavy for the drainpipe," he pointed out.

It was sweet of him to worry, but climbing down drainpipes was half her job description on an average day. "I'll be alright, you'll see."

It took a few seconds for Bob to wrap his head around what she had just said, squinting his eyes as if to imagine her climbing down the wall Spider-Man style. Stephanie gave him all the time he needed, simply grateful he was willing to help.

Eventually, he turned and walked to his bedroom. Stephanie followed quietly.

Once at the window, Bob opened it and let the cold February breeze rush in. Stephanie glanced at the sixteen-foot drop to the back garden below, high enough to hurt, especially someone who had just recovered from being blown up by an exploding spacecraft. The drainpipe was to her right, hanging to the wall like a lifeline, exactly where she knew it would be.

"One more thing before I go," she said, turning to him. "If these people ask about me, I want you to tell them I forced you to help me. Could you do that for me?"

There was more disappointment than protest on Bob's face as he asked, "You want me to tell a lie?"

Stephanie silently reproached herself for not thinking it through. She hung her head, acknowledging the mistake. "I know. You don't like telling lies. Maybe just don't tell them anything about this. At all. Can you do that?"

He nodded, although his scrunched-up face revealed how

little he knew how to make that work without lying. "Are you going to be gone long?" he asked.

"I don't know," she replied in earnest. She wished she didn't have to go at all. Resting a hand on Bob's shoulder, she gently pulled him into a hug. As his arms wrapped around her, she squeezed tight. "I'm sorry, big boy. It'll be over soon."

He pulled back from the hug slowly. "Be careful out there, Steph."

"I will."

Before the lump in her throat could turn into actual tears, Stephanie pulled the duffle bag onto the window ledge and looked below. Then, she pushed the bag into the open air, watching as it landed on the grass with a soft thud.

My turn now, she thought.

It was only as she stepped on the ledge that it occurred to her how her left arm might not be fit enough for free climbing. Even so, it was the left arm she stretched out first to get a grip on the drainpipe as she swung a leg over the window ledge and turned her face against the wall.

She held her breath as a sharp pain ran through her forearm. Only when she felt the left foot solidly anchored on the drainpipe support, she allowed herself to exhale.

Now to hope Bob hasn't jinxed it and the supports don't give, she thought.

As she pulled the right arm and leg away from the window, she redistributed her weight, making sure to bear on the supports rather than hanging from the drainpipe itself. A few moments later, she touched the ground with a sigh of relief.

She leaned against the wall to catch her breath, waiting for the pain to subside. When she glanced at the duffle bag, all she could think was that she hadn't packed any painkillers while raiding her own apartment.

There was little time to linger, though. Stephanie went to pick up the bag and looked up at the window. Bob was still standing there. She waved at him.

He gave her a big smile and a thumbs-up.

Time to move on. Over the fence and onto the walkway that separated the neighbouring house gardens, Stephanie made her way to the road. She wasn't sure whether Victoria's men were going to search the area or rely exclusively on the tracking device that they had put on her. Either way, she could use it to her advantage.

She spotted the bus stop in the distance and sped up to a jog to reach the awning as the bus pulled to the kerb. There was just time to get the tracker out of her pocket and step inside.

"Hey, is this going to Hengrove?" she asked the driver, knowing full well it wasn't. She only half-listened to the response, letting the tracker drop to a corner of the floor. "Right, thanks," she said as the driver's gesturing stopped.

Once off the bus, she pulled her hood over her head and started walking.

* * *

It was almost surprising to see Roxy hadn't replaced the lock on her front door since the last time they spoke. It had been a whole two years since she had been posted to the Middle East in another SafeOp sensitive mission.

Before that, that house had been their home.

Memories best left alone, Stephanie decided.

She swept the pile of mail to the side and made her way in.

She navigated the house as if she had never left, turning the heating on, running the tap and rinsing the kettle before turning it on to make a brew, and opening cupboards to find familiar mugs. Half an hour later, she felt warm and comfortable enough for her to take her jacket off.

Sat at the kitchen table, warming her hands around a steam-ing cup of tea, she waited for Roxy's laptop to connect to the Wi-Fi.

She was all set.

With Gwyn still alive and the Cavell family up to their necks in the Avis Carmen's machinations, the first thing on Stephanie's agenda was to find Frank and Lucy Campbell. They had to be warned and kept safe.

The Cavell family had to wait. She wasn't going to poke the hornets' nest until she was sure the Campbells were out of their reach.

While Lucy could be hard to trace, Frank offered a more solid lead at the University of Bristol, where he had been taking his PhD the last time she saw him. A few weeks couldn't have changed much. He was likely still there.

Checking the events calendar for the Chemistry Department soon gave Stephanie a lucky break. A seminar was scheduled in only a few days, and Frank was mentioned in the list of speakers.

* * *

On the morning of the seminar, Stephanie planned for an early start. Making her way up the hill to the Department of Chemistry, a few variables remained unpredictable. For one, it was possible Victoria was keeping Frank under surveillance, just as she had tried to do with her.

Stephanie felt in her pocket for the keys. She had decided not to carry weapons, but the keys between her knuckles made for a killer punch of the most literal kind.

Once she reached the main entrance to the department, she picked a spot to the side from which she could survey the area, then took out a book on the history of chemistry she had found in Roxy's bookcase. She might not have passed for a student, but at least she wouldn't look exceedingly suspicious.

It was a cold half hour later that the slim figure of Frank Campbell made an appearance. He was looking straight ahead, chin held high, confident in his stride.

Stephanie caught up with him, bent down as if picking up something, then brushed his arm. "Excuse me, sir. I think you dropped something."

Frank turned around, and surprise washed over his face as he recognised her. Before he could say anything, though, she resumed talking. "Don't say a word. Follow me."

She rushed him behind the corner before he burst, "You're alive!"

Stephanie cautioned him to be quiet, hoping nobody had noticed the unusual utterance.

"You're alive," he repeated in a somewhat softer tone.

"Yes, we've established that," she replied. "What about you? How have you been doing? How's Lucy?"

"I'm fine. We're all fine," he replied hurriedly, then leaned forward to touch Stephanie's arm, as if needing reassurance of her tangible presence. "You're really here. We thought you died."

She didn't like the uninvited touch, although did her best not to show it. "Yeah, well. I walked it off," she dismissed him quickly. "You guys okay? Life back to normal?"

Frank removed his hand from Stephanie's arm and averted

his eyes. "Yeah, back to normal, of course. No more alien creepy crawlies running around, that's for sure."

His chuckle at the end was awkward as he stole a glance at her before focusing on something somewhere over Stephanie's right shoulder. He was lying, and he was being terrible at it.

"And is Lucy doing okay?" she asked tentatively. "She was dating that guy when I last saw her. Matthew, was it?"

A coy attempt to see how close to danger they all were. Frank took a second to answer, as if he had to decide what to say and what to keep hidden. "She's great, yes. They moved in together, actually. She's good. We're good."

There was nothing good about it, and it didn't take an expert to sense it. It looked like Matthew Cavell – and Avis Carmen with him – was already three steps ahead in the recruitment process.

While she processed all that, though, Frank still had questions of his own. "How did you survive?" he was asking.

"Good Samaritan came along, patched me up, and here I am," she replied quickly, suddenly aware how she didn't know the answer to that question herself. She shrugged the thought away. "Listen, there's something I need you to know."

Frank didn't wait for her to continue. "The Skaara is alive, I know."

It was Stephanie's turn to recoil in surprise. "How do you know that?"

"As I said, my sister moved in with my best friend, and his family is into all sorts of things, including space aliens," he said, then his expression changed, as if he had just had a revelation. "You should meet them! I'm sure they'd love to work with you."

Stephanie smiled politely. "Thanks for the offer, but you know I work best on my own."

"There are things you can't do on your own."

He wasn't entirely wrong. Some things were best taken down from the inside, after all. "I'll think about it, okay?"

Frank gave her the first genuine smile of the day. "Let me give you my number so we can keep in touch."

"I don't really do phones these days," she replied, stopping him halfway through pulling his phone out of his pocket. "I'll know how to find you."

"Right. Okay."

Stephanie heard the disappointment in Frank's tone. She chose to ignore it and glanced around the corner to see that the morning crowd had already dispersed.

"I have to go," she said, then stalked across the lawn before he could reply.

* * *

Clouds had gathered after the morning's sunny spell. It was the kind of weather that made it hard to believe days were getting longer as spring crept closer.

Stephanie took the keys to the front door from her pocket. The train rattled behind her on its way around the city.

She didn't need to take more than a step inside to realise something was wrong – someone was there.

The jacket on the coat hanger by the door didn't look familiar, so Stephanie felt confident excluding Victoria from the possible visitors. That left several dangerous alternatives.

She readied herself, keys in her hands should she have needed a weapon, then stepped gingerly down the hall and towards the living room door. The figure she spotted sitting on the sofa was not what she expected.

"Roxy?"

The figure straightened up and turned towards the door. "Hey, love. I hope you don't mind, I let myself in."

Her hair was shorter, and she had an undercut that made her look like a character from a comic book story. Her sunglasses were drawn over her head, and she held a bottle of beer that Stephanie didn't remember being in the fridge. "What are you doing here?" she asked.

"It's my house, honey," replied Roxy with a shrug. "The right question is, what are *you* doing here?"

- V -

The front door opened and quickly slammed shut. Lucy looked up from her book, trying to remember if Matthew said he would return early from work or if she should have grabbed something heavy to throw at the intruder.

Then Frank's voice came from the hall, "Matthew!"

Lucy put down her paperback copy of *The Seven Husbands of Evelyn Hugo*. "I hate to disappoint," she called out.

Still intent on taking his gloves off, Frank stepped into the living room. "Oh good, you're here. You'll never believe what happened."

"Try me," she replied.

He struggled to take off his coat as he continued, "I was on my way to the lab. I wanted to sort out my notes before the seminar this afternoon, and it's a good thing I did because—"

"You came here to tell me about your seminar?" interrupted Lucy.

Frank looked at her wide-eyed. "It's Stephanie."

Lucy stared at him transfixed. That was a name she hadn't expected to hear again. She felt a lump rising to her throat, and the memory of all she had done to cause Stephanie Davis's death washed over her. She looked away from her brother, wishing the conversation away. "She's dead, Frankie. It doesn't matter if your whole seminar was about her."

"She's alive," he countered. "And the seminar wasn't about her, anyway."

Lucy shook her head. "That's not possible."

She had already been through that. After weeks of scanning the news for scraps of information, and jumping at the sound of each phone notifications, she had finally come to terms with Davis's death. She had accepted the truth, and she had done her grieving.

She opened her book again, set on ignoring her brother until he disappeared from her sight.

Frank, however, was stubbornly keeping around. "She made it out," he insisted, stepping into the living room like an invading force for the disruption of her reality. "Somehow, she survived and came to find me this morning. I saw her, and I talked to her. She's as alive as you and I are. I swear."

Lucy stared at him. The book still open in her lap. His words swam through the air around her.

She wasn't even sure she recognised the feeling curling in her chest: she was relieved and fearful; happy and angry; hurt and confused. The bundle of emotions was tightening in her throat, so she hurried to speak while she still could. "What did she want?"

He shrugged. "Just to know if we were okay. I don't know," he replied. "She knew about Gwyn."

"Is she working with Matthew's parents?" she asked, dreading to hear that Davis was part of that stupid Avis Carmen plot too.

Frank shook his head. "No. She said she works best on her own."

Good to see her hero complex is also alive and well, thought Lucy, a tight smile pulling at her lips. "Yeah, that sounds like her."

A moment of awkward hesitation, then Lucy watched Frank pick up his coat. "I have to go back to the lab. I just wanted to give you the news. Oh, and I wanted to give you this. Sorry I kept it so long."

He took something from his pocket and threw it across the room.

Lucy watched as the object dropped on the carpet, landing between the armchair and the wall to her left – her pink sloth keyring. She stared at the furry flash drive for a long moment, almost unable to comprehend its presence in her hand. Her mind was stuck on Davis's return to the land of the living. "Thanks," she managed. "Do you think she'll be in touch again?"

Frank shrugged. "Maybe? She's not doing phones these days, so she must be lying low or something. I'm sure she'll be in touch if she needs to. See you later, Luce."

He hesitated on the threshold, however Lucy's mind was miles away from responding. Eventually, he turned and left.

As the front door closed on the silent apartment, Lucy sank back into the armchair. Tears started pouring down her cheeks, like a flood she had been holding back for months, and that she could hardly contain by bringing her hands to her face.

For minutes, she let it all out. Not because she wanted, but because she couldn't help it. She had carried the guilt for causing Davis's death for months, and the weight had almost broken her. With that heavy burden suddenly lifted, Lucy found herself exposed and more vulnerable than she had ever felt before.

Unexpectedly, a grin spread across her face. *Davis is alive*, she thought.

Tears still streaming down her face, Lucy started to laugh until she had run out of both tears and laughter. She closed her eyes and tilted her head back, taking a deep breath. Her mind was reeling, adrenaline rushing through her. She removed the book from her lap and went to pick up the pink sloth her brother had thrown at her.

It felt like a world of possibilities had just opened before her.

For days, she hadn't stopped thinking about Matthew's behaviour at Uncle Jim's. She had been trying to tune the noise out and pretend it was none of her business, but she couldn't go on ignoring the alien elephant in the room much longer.

Davis would have known what to do about it. She would've known how to handle the whole alien elephant and then some.

Lucy left the living room and went to the bedroom. She hadn't looked at the black box – *the beacon*, she reminded herself – since they had returned from the visit to Uncle Jim. She had tucked it in a corner behind the wardrobe until she could figure out what to do with it. Her fingers found it again where she had left it.

She undid the wrapping, and sure enough, the beacon was still emitting that deep, intermittent blackness.

She should have thrown the thing away as soon as she had found it. Lucy wondered what would happen if she threw it in the Avon River there and then, watching it float away from her. She could've left Matthew and moved back to Sophie. She could've left Bristol and started over somewhere else, away from all that Skaara madness that kept on following her around.

She had done that before, when she had left her childhood home in small-town Axminster in the middle of the night to start anew in Bristol. She could have done it again.

Except that Davis was alive, and it was Davis that had made

her see how there wouldn't be a place away from the Skaara anywhere on Earth, unless someone did something about it.

Not that Lucy was the only person who would be taking a stand. She was sure Davis was already planning and scheming, hero style. However, Davis didn't have the beacon, nor inside access to the Avis Carmen operation.

Lucy wrapped the beacon tightly in the newspaper once again and pushed the pink sloth deep into her pocket.

She didn't know where to find Davis, but knew where to start. They had a lot to catch up on.

* * *

A crackling voice came through the intercom soon after she had pressed the doorbell. "Hello?"

"Hi, my name is Lucy. I'm Davis's friend," she said, then quickly corrected herself, "Stephanie. I'm Stephanie's friend."

A short silence, then the voice again. "She's not home."

"Do you mind if I come up anyway?"

Another short silence. "Are you one of them agents?"

Them agents must have been people from the Avis Carmen operation. Either that or Davis got herself in a lot more trouble than Lucy had expected.

A sudden blast of cold wind hit her, and she wrapped herself tighter in her jacket, though with no real improvement. "If I was, I wouldn't bother ringing the doorbell, don't you think?" she countered, giving in to frustration. "I'm her friend, I swear. Can you please let me in? It's freezing out here."

The door buzzed open, and Lucy let herself into the entrance hall. As she paused to consider her next move, she remembered the nosy ground–floor neighbour from her previous visit. She had kept watch on her as if she had been a fugitive from justice. Eager to avoid a repeat of that treatment, Lucy made a dash for the stairs just as the old lady opened the door. "Don't you think I didn't see you!" the woman cried, then went on mumbling to herself as she walked back into her apartment.

Stepping on the first-floor landing, however, Lucy was too distracted to worry about that, as a large young man with a bushy beard was waiting. "Steph is not home."

"I know," she said. "I'm trying to find her. Do you know where she is?"

"Your name is Lucy," he said.

"Yes, Lucy Campbell. And you are?"

"Bob."

He stepped back into his flat and gestured to follow. As soon as they were inside, he closed the door and bolted it, then walked away from Lucy and to the living room ahead.

"Nice to meet you, Bob," she whispered, suddenly unsure what to do with herself while in the presence of Bob the Friendly Giant.

She followed him into the apartment, sensing his distrust. In the corner of the living room, a LEGO reproduction of the Millennium Falcon took up most of the table. Bob stood next to it, gently turning the laser cannon as if he were adjusting its aim.

"It has seven thousand five hundred and forty-one pieces," he said. I wanted to show Steph, but she was in a hurry."

While appreciating the LEGO Falcon, Lucy had no time to spend on it. She tried to keep her tone level as she asked. "Why was she in a hurry?"

He gave her a sideway glance and bit his lip, as if realising he had said too much.

"It was the agent people, wasn't it?" she guessed.

Bob nodded.

"I'm not one of them, Bob."

A thick silence fell between them as Bob picked up the Chewbacca piece, cradling it in his hands, like he was holding his most precious possession. "Did you know that Chewbacca's voice was made up of a mixture of badger, lion, seal, and walrus calls?"

Lucy tried not to sound too puzzled by the unsolicited sharing of Star Wars trivia. "Right," she managed. "That's interesting."

"Wookies don't have lips like humans do, so they had to figure out a way for them to talk," he clarified.

There was no telling why he was talking to her about Star Wars. Lucy wanted to get back to the point and ask about Davis, but she was getting the impression that insisting on that point wouldn't get her anywhere. If talking about Star Wars was the way into Bob's trust circle, she had to give it a shot. Fortunately, she was enough of a fan to carry a conversation about it. "I always wondered how people could understand what he said."

"Most people didn't," he explained.

She walked closer and identified one of the LEGO figures on top of the Falcon. She pointed at it, careful not to touch it. "Han Solo did," she said. "I bet it's the same between you and Steph. You care for her because she understands you."

Bob sneaked a glance at her, then placed the Chewbacca figure back in its place. "I don't know where she went," he said. "She didn't want the agent people to find her."

Back on the subject. Finally.

"Do you know how to get in touch with her?" she asked. "There's something really important I have to tell her."

He shook his head. "She told me not to say anything, so I don't have to tell lies."

There wasn't much time for Lucy to process what that could mean as a loud knock came at the front door, followed by an authoritative voice. "Mr Colton! Would you mind opening the door, please? This is Victoria. We met before!"

There was terror in Bob's eyes as he stepped back against the wall. Lucy took no time thinking about what to do. "I'll talk to her," she said. "I'll take her away from you."

His eyes locked onto her. There was a glint of uncertainty and a spark of hope. It made Lucy want to tell him that everything would be okay, but lying to him felt wrong.

Is that what being like Davis feels like? Lucy wasn't enjoying that too much.

Victoria called out again just as Lucy reached the front door and opened it. She glared at the short, round woman, who stood alone on the landing yet held her position as if she were a team of five.

Lucy was not going to be intimidated. "Step into this flat, and the Cavells will hear about it."

It was a gamble to throw the name out like that, and for a moment, Lucy feared she might have misjudged what team this Victoria was playing for – or how powerful her boyfriend's name really was.

"Who am I speaking to?" the woman asked, suddenly cautious.

"Not here," said Lucy, stepping out of Bob's flat and closing the door behind her. "I believe Davis's apartment is empty. Shall we talk there?"

Victoria nodded and led the way upstairs, where she produced a key to Davis's flat and opened the door. Inside, everything was just like Lucy remembered, except the sofa had been pushed closer to the wall, and the temperature was much colder.

She sat on the same stool she had chosen that evening a lifetime before, when she had visited a Skaara-controlled Agent Davis. Part of her almost expected her to magically appear on the other side of the kitchen.

Instead, Victoria stood opposite her.

The woman's face looked familiar. It took a few seconds for Lucy to remember where they had met before. "You helped Gwyn at the landing site."

"And you were supposed to take her cargo out of there instead of driving away as it exploded," replied Victoria. "Why are you here, Campbell?"

No, Lucy wasn't going to tell her that. "Same reason you are," she bluffed.

"I don't think so!" countered Victoria. "You're here because you don't know where Davis is, and I'm sure it wasn't any of the Cavells who sent you here. So, why would you want to find her?"

For a spy, Victoria wasn't very good at keeping secrets. Lucy let a sly smile rise to her lips. "I wanted to leave some flowers on her grave, but it seems I'm a bit early for that."

The two women studied each other for a moment. Eventually, it was Victoria who broke the silence. "Listen, we're all working towards the same goal! Me, you, even Davis. However, as you know, Stephanie has a mind of her own, and it might take a while before she comes round to accept that!"

"Do you know where she is?"

"Of course!"

"Are you going to tell me?" insisted Lucy.

Victoria scoffed at the idea. "No!"

Lucy exhaled, her hands going to her pockets. The beacon's edge grazed her knuckles, giving her an idea – risky, but worth a try. "Okay, let's try another way," she said. "I suppose you heard about a black box. It's said to have disappeared from Mr Cavell's safe. It was quite important, wasn't it?"

"You know about the beacon," said Victoria. "Yes, its disappearance caused quite a stir."

Resting her elbows on the counter, Lucy leaned forward. Her voice was close to a whisper as she said, "Yes, I know about the beacon, and I know Davis has it hidden away somewhere. I can get it from her. You just have to tell me where she is."

In response to her conspiratorial stance, Victoria sneered. "Why aren't you telling this to the Cavells, I wonder? Unless, of course, your boyfriend has no idea you're even here!" She paused for effect, then added, "I'm not that easily fooled, as you can see."

While trying not to react to Victoria's provocation, Lucy felt her heartbeat quicken in her chest. "I don't tell everything to my boyfriend," she said icily. "Do you tell everything to your boss?"

Some hesitation before Victoria lightly shook her head and asked, "Why would she listen to you?"

"Because she will think I'm on her side," explained Lucy.

Victoria's tone had become hushed, matching Lucy's wariness of listening ears. "Davis doesn't believe anyone is on her side."

"Keeping her apartment under surveillance doesn't exactly scream *friendly*, does it?" replied Lucy. "Maybe we could try a more human approach. Tell me where she is. Let me talk to her."

There was a short pause, then Victoria sagged over the

counter, resting her weight on her forearms as if she was going to topple down any second. "I can't take surveillance off her. She's too much of a contingency..." she trailed off, then exhaled. She looked as if she knew something terrible was going to happen, and she had no way to prevent it.

Lucy wouldn't have believed it if someone had told her, but Victoria seemed to actually care about Davis.

"She's like a dog with a bone," said Lucy. "I remember Edward Cook saying that about her. Which means that, if you take the beacon from her, she'll just keep on coming with her personal hero plan to stop Avis Carmen from doing anything."

Victoria nodded, her head still bent down. "Avis Carmen will have no use for her once the beacon has been retrieved."

It was what Lucy expected to hear, yet that didn't make it any easier to digest.

I'm not going to let her die again, she thought. "We both want the same thing, Victoria. Just tell me where she is."

With a final sigh, the woman lifted herself from the counter and straightened her spine in a show of resolution. "I can't do that, and you should stop asking."

It looked as if she was about to say something else when her phone rang in her pocket. She took it out only to reject the call and slide the smartphone back in its place.

The movement lasted a second, but it was enough to give Lucy an idea.

She stood up from her stool and dipped her hands in her pockets. "Fine," she said, sprinkling some drama in her voice. "I don't want to waste your time, nor mine. You're clearly not going to help me, so I won't insist any longer. Let's just try not to get in the way of each other. Do you agree?"

Victoria was staring at her, and Lucy feared she had underestimated how sceptical the woman would be of her change of heart. Before there could be enough time for that scepticism to produce any conclusive theory, Lucy circled the counter in a few swift strides. Victoria's unblinking stare followed her all the way, her eyes widening in something close to horror when Lucy placed herself in front of her, arms wide open, and said, "How about we hug it out before I leave you be?"

She didn't wait for a response. Lucy's arms wrapped around Victoria's shoulders and squeezed. The shock of the situation must have paralysed the woman, as she stiffened for a few seconds in protest before regaining control of herself and trying to wriggle away. "What are you doing? Let go of me," she mumbled.

Lucy promptly stepped away. Her objective accomplished, she held her hands in the air as a sign of surrender. "Fine, fine. No touchy, I get it. I'll be out of your air, then."

She turned and walked out of the flat before Victoria could react, hoping the shock would still linger, and that her moves had been sudden enough for her not to realise what was happening.

As soon as she was out of the flat, the door securely closed behind her, Lucy rushed down the stairs and out into the street. The bus stop was only a few minutes' walk away. Lucy turned the corner to see the shape of a bus making its way towards the awning. She couldn't let it go by without her.

She made a run for it and reached the bus doors just as the driver was about to press the button to close them. She hopped on board and took her place in a lonely seat at the back of the bus, past an old woman in a baggy winter coat and a couple of girls covered in enough piercings to restock a jewellery store. Most importantly, none of them was interested in Lucy.

She relaxed against the backseat and glanced out the window

to see Victoria's figure in the distance, just reaching the bus stop – too late.

A nervous grin on her lips, Lucy fished into her pockets. In her right hand, Victoria's phone was securely locked. In her left hand, her own phone recognised her face and willingly offered its services to her.

The number she needed to call was one she hadn't used in a long time.

A groggy voice answered on the third ring. "Luce? The fuck are you calling for? Are you okay?"

"Hey, Wally! Sorry, I couldn't wait for you to wake up and read a text." She glanced around warily at the other passengers. She'd need to measure her words carefully. "I got a new phone and need your help getting it to work."

There was a sigh on the other end of the line. Lucy wondered if Walter would hang up on her or if he'd spell out the words *piss off* first. Instead, he said, "Of course you do. Come down. You still know where I live, right?"

As she ended the call, Lucy watched the next bus stop approach.

Victoria knew what bus she had taken, and it couldn't be long before she put someone on her tail.

She pressed the button to request the stop, then made her way to the exit.

The microwave beeped, and Stephanie went to get the freshly warmed soup – chicken and coriander, the same one her mum used to make when she was sick as a child. Not something she'd call a fond memory.

She sat down at the table. In front of her were the newest additions to her toolbox, in the shape of a burner phone and a pay-as-you-go SIM card she had registered in the name of Amelie Renard.

As if summoned by the smell, Roxy strode through the kitchen door, holding a stack of road atlases in her arms. "You made enough for two?" she asked, dropping the pile of paper on the table.

"There's some more in the fridge if you want it," replied Stephanie, struggling to open the SIM compartment of the GSM phone. She felt Roxy's eyes on her, silently judging her failure to bend an old device to her wishes. "It would be easier without an audience."

Roxy shrugged and walked to the fridge just as the compartment gave in, and Stephanie successfully slid the SIM card into the slot.

Meanwhile, Roxy had found the second portion of soup and entrusted it to the microwave. "Where are you planning to go, anyway?" she asked, nodding towards the atlases still untouched on the table.

Stephanie shrugged. "Still figuring it out."

Stephanie pressed the button to switch on the mobile phone. Just as the screen lit up, someone knocked at the door.

The two women looked at each other. None of them was expecting guests.

Even if Victoria had managed to track her down, it was too bold a move to be knocking at her door like that. Stephanie grabbed the gun and released the safety while Roxy made her way down the hall.

Stephanie remained seated at the table, holding her breath, waiting for voices to waft down the corridor.

She started when the visitor knocked again, following up with, "Davis? I can see your shadow."

Lucy Campbell.

Not something Stephanie had expected.

As Roxy opened the door, Stephanie silently rose from her seat and walked to the kitchen door, careful to remain unseen.

"Can I help you?" Roxy asked, and Stephanie could picture her holding the door ajar, her left hand holding her gun, hidden behind the doorframe.

Lucy's voice was meek when she spoke. "Oh. You're not Davis."

"Glad we agree. Bye–bye, girl."

Roxy was already closing the door when Stephanie stepped out in the hall. "Wait."

The look on Roxy's face was pure disbelief. She furrowed her brow and pointed at the girl still standing behind the door, as if asking, "This one? Really?"

Stephanie shrugged, and Roxy opened the door wide. Lucy

stood on the threshold, her winter jacket making her look twice as large as herself.

"Hey," she said, a grin spreading on her face.

The relief she felt in seeing her was more than Stephanie had expected. She pushed the emotion aside as soon as she felt it flooding her chest. "Are you going to come in, or are we waiting for the cavalry to show up and shoot us?"

The smile on Lucy's face disappeared. "Yes, ma'am," she said as she marched inside.

Roxy promptly closed the door behind her. "I suppose I should give you two a minute," she said, then sidled up the stairs and out of the way.

"How did you find me here?" asked Stephanie once Roxy had disappeared.

"I'm glad to see you too," replied Lucy. "At least this time you're not holding me at gunpoint. We're making progress."

Stephanie didn't know what to think. On the one hand, she was annoyed at how irresponsible Lucy had been in showing up that way; on the other, it was impressive how the girl had found out where she was.

"You want tea?" Stephanie asked as she turned and walked back to the kitchen.

She didn't turn to check if Lucy was following, but she heard her just behind her as she murmured, "I'm glad to see you alive too."

Ignoring the sarcasm, Stephanie turned on the kettle, then took her position against the kitchen counter, arms crossed on her chest. "How did you find me?"

"A little birdy told me," replied Lucy, then sniffed the air, glancing across the table to Stephanie's untouched dinner. "Is that coriander soup? Are you sick or something?"

Stephanie barely raised an eyebrow, waiting for a real answer. The girl, however, wasn't going to concede. "See you got yourself a bodyguard," she remarked with a sneer, then nodded at road atlases on the table, "and you picked up cartography?"

Stephanie did her best to conceal a smile at the joke. "Not a bodyguard, and not a hobby. How did you find me?" she insisted.

The sneer had disappeared from Lucy's face. "Well, you went to talk to my brother, didn't you?"

The beep of the microwave punctuated the short silence that followed. Stephanie opened the door to prevent it from disturbing their conversation.

She had suspected Frank Campbell might be under surveillance. That still didn't explain the visit, though. She had expected Lucy to do her best to stay out of all that – unless she had already been recruited into the Avis Carmen scheme.

"Why are you here?"

Lucy clenched her fists. When she spoke, her words were drenched in sarcasm. "I missed you very much," she said, her lips tight in a smile that wouldn't quite reach her eyes.

Stephanie exhaled. The way she had welcomed Lucy had probably deserved her that treatment. "I see joining a cult hasn't ruined your sense of humour."

The comment hit a soft spot Stephanie hadn't expected to be there. Lucy broke eye contact and crossed her arms on her chest. "I..." she started, but the rest of the sentence seemed stuck somewhere in her throat. She exhaled instead, then sank into one of the chairs. "I have no idea what I'm doing here. I needed to see you."

If that was an act, it was Academy-worthy. Stephanie sat on the chair next to Lucy, one arm resting on the table, inviting her to talk. "Go on."

"Matthew is great," started Lucy, with the same tone she'd use to confess her sins to the vicar. "He's nice, sweet, and gets extra marshmallows in my hot chocolate. And Frankie adores him, which is almost ridiculous at times." She paused before continuing, "I don't like this Avis Carmen business he's in. I don't like what his family is doing, and I don't like how he behaves about it. I don't like how much he believes in it. Most of all, I don't like how he dragged Frank into that too."

Stephanie waited, confident that Lucy hadn't just come by to tell the troubles of her heart. Eventually, her patience was rewarded. "Gwyn is their prisoner, just like she has been a prisoner before. They're probably experimenting on her just the same. I don't know. I just want to do the right thing this time, without getting someone killed."

If only Stephanie had known what the right thing to do was. "What makes you think they're keeping her prisoner?"

Lucy shrugged. "It's the way they talk about it. They're saying the Skaara are sending a warship. I bet squeezing Gwyn for information is part of their plan to protect the world, or however they like to put it."

That all checked with what Victoria had told her. "Do you know where they're keeping her?" she asked.

Lucy shook her head. "I know where to find the comms guy, if that helps."

Stephanie frowned, unsure how that could be relevant. "Who's the comms guy?"

"Matthew's uncle was the first to contact the Skaara years ago. When he told his sister, she hijacked the discovery and set up the Avis Carmen operation. Uncle Jim didn't like what she wanted to do, so he moved out of the way to Macclesfield, never to be seen again, until Matthew drove us there last week and convinced him to join Avis Carmen after all."

Absorbing the story with a nod, Stephanie took a moment to think. The comms guy had to be a crucial part of the puzzle. "What do you think changed his mind?" she asked.

Lucy shifted her weight on the chair. "That's the thing. I don't know," she started, drawing her hands together to trace the lines of her palms as if they held the answers she needed. "One moment, we're in the kitchen, and Jim is telling me how he loathes the whole organisation. Then Matthew comes in to have a private chat, and five minutes later, the family is back together again."

A private chat. The scenario didn't leave much room for imagination. "Your boyfriend blackmailed him."

As soon as she said the words, Stephanie realised how insensitive they must have sounded. Lucy leaned her arms on the table, her head in her hands. She looked exhausted and vulnerable.

"Yeah," she exhaled.

"Do you think Uncle Jim might still be on our side?"

Lucy dropped one of her arms to show a grimace in response. "There's something else I wanted to show you," she then said, straightening up and pulling out of her pocket the pink furry sloth – the same keyring Stephanie had taken from her a long time before, only to let her take it back with the Skaara's blessing.

"I recognise the little fella," she commented.

Lucy twisted its head to reveal the flash drive underneath. She held it up as if she had just performed a magic trick.

"Am I supposed to be impressed?"

Lucy gave her a disappointed look. "You already knew."

"I suspected. What's inside?"

"A bunch of photos and videos that I'd invite you to never open," replied Lucy, "plus all the results your ex-employer gathered while experimenting on Gwyn."

That was somewhat impressive. Stephanie reached out her hand to receive the gift. "Why are you giving it to me?"

"I gave it to my brother before leaving the landing site, thinking it'd be safe with him. Now he gave it back, and I think it'd be best to keep it away from me."

Away from Matthew, she means.

The Avis Carmen team had likely already extracted all that information from the sequestered Skaara, yet Stephanie understood Lucy's fear of keeping that information at hand. "If I'm right, they had infiltrated SafeOp way before you or I were involved. That flash drive won't tell them anything they don't already know," she said, trying to be reassuring. "Still, I could use the intel. Thank you."

A serious look of alarm appeared on Lucy's face. "Hold on, did you say they infiltrated SafeOp? As in the agency you worked for?"

The shocked reaction was unexpected. "I don't have proof, but it's safe to assume so," she explained with a measured tone. "In any case, the agency has been dissolved, so it doesn't make much difference now."

That was a lie, and Stephanie hoped Lucy wouldn't notice. She could hardly reveal how Roxy had been on SafeOp's payroll until only a few weeks earlier, and there was still no evidence to show ex-Director Millican hadn't recruited her into Avis Carmen already. She could have been sent back home to spy on Stephanie and keep her in check for all she knew.

Stephanie felt no need to tell Lucy any of that. In an attempt to shift the attention, Stephanie raised the pink sloth and asked,

"Do you think Frank saw what's in here?"

Lucy seemed reluctant to change the subject. She opened her mouth to protest, but Stephanie insisted on keeping the flash drive in the spotlight. Rolling her eyes, Lucy responded, "I don't know. He didn't say. I'd assume he has."

Stephanie agreed that was likely. Frank might even have used the information to gain some station within Avis Carmen.

Clearly uninterested in talking about her brother, Lucy sagged back in her chair and reached into her pocket. "I have one last Christmas present for you," she said, then produced a small parcel wrapped in a newspaper.

Stephanie took the box and eyed it suspiciously. "You got me a present?" she asked with half a smile, hoping the joke would go some length in cheering Lucy up. It didn't.

"Just open it," the girl said.

She unfolded the wrapping. A black shape appeared underneath the folds of the newspaper, although *black* didn't feel like a strong enough word to describe the colour of the small object – and that wasn't even the eeriest thing about it. The more she looked at it, the more she perceived a pulse, as if it was intermittently getting darker every few seconds. "Do you think it's transmitting something?" she asked.

"Why would you say it's transmitting anything?"

"In my line of work, when things pulse like this, it's either a bomb or a transmitter," explained Stephanie. "I've had enough explosions for a couple of lifetimes, so I'm very much hoping it's a transmitter."

"Uncle Jim said it's a beacon."

"Like a homing beacon?" she asked.

Lucy, however, wasn't wiser to it than she was. "Maybe?" she said, accompanying the interrogative tone with a shrug.

Stephanie nodded, turning the box in her hands. "I'll take it back. I'd rather it was a bomb."

Lucy, however, wasn't following. "What's bad about it being a beacon?"

"The Skaara are sending a warship, and this is a beacon," she explained. "A homing beacon, like the one they placed in Scotland for Gwyn to follow."

The small object wasn't bigger than a can of Coke. She turned it in her hands, trying to find any dent in the structure, anything that might look like a button to deactivate the signal. The object, however, was a single smooth, uninterrupted surface. "Can you tell me where to find Uncle Jim?"

"Yes," said Lucy, springing into action as she reached for her phone. "I checked the journey before we left."

Stephanie stared at her, horrified at the sight of the smart-phone in her hands. "You did not just walk in here with a built-in GPS tracker."

Lucy looked up, a confounded gaze that only lasted a moment. "Oh, this?" she said, hinting at her phone. "I wouldn't worry. They already know you're here. I took this address from Evans's phone."

Sources of amazement seemed to be endless with Lucy. "You mean she gave it to you?"

"I took her phone," explained Lucy with a shrug, then added quickly, "Don't worry about that. I threw it in the river before coming here. She has no evidence it was me who stole it."

Somehow, Stephanie didn't find that reassuring. Lack of evidence wasn't going to stop retaliation. However, before she could express her indignation at Lucy's recklessness, a grin spread on the girl's face as she burst, "There! Still in my search history. Macclesfield. Do you know where it is?"

Stephanie took a moment to decide how deliberate was Lucy's ignorance of the gravity of her actions. Eventually, she shook her head and opted to move on. The damage was done. Arguing about it wasn't going to make it any better.

From the pile of road atlases on the table, she picked the one that covered the north of the country.

"You're joking, right?" said Lucy. She was staring at the book as if it were a satanic relic.

Stephanie glanced at her. "Would you rather I used a GPS device to go talk to the person your boyfriend blackmailed on behalf of his very own family cult? Boy, I do hope they put some surveillance on him, or I might just get out of it alive. Then again, you just walked in here with that, so why am I bothering."

Lucy lifted a hand as a defence towards the wave of sarcasm. "Fine, you're right. Better use the archaic treasure map for this one. Here, this is the place. Make sure you put an X to mark the spot."

On the screen of Lucy's phone, Stephanie checked the address and the location of the house, then found the coordinates on the atlas. "Macclesfield is easy enough to get to, and the house is in an isolated enough area. It should be okay. I'll make my way in the morning."

"Cool," burst Lucy, slapping her hands on her thighs as she stood up. "Should I meet you here, or would you rather pick me up somewhere else?"

Stephanie gave her a blank stare. Lucy couldn't possibly believe she was going with her. "Listen," she started, slowly standing up as she tried to find the right words to tell her how much of a liability she would be. "I'm very grateful for the intel and the pulsing box of doom here, but this is not a team-up.

I'm going alone."

Lucy, however, stood unwavering. "You mean like that time I had to lure Gwyn out of the hangar so that you wouldn't get caught fixing the explosives *on your own*?"

"Yes," Stephanie snapped, remembering full well that wasn't the whole story. "The same explosives that almost killed me while I was trying to clean up the mess you started in the first place. Or have you forgotten who snuck the alien out of the SafeOp laboratory?"

Lucy's expression hardened. "That's beside the point, and you know it. Not to mention, they were torturing her."

"Are you trying to tell me you did that out of the kindness of your heart?"

"No, I did it to save myself and my brother from that place!"

"By setting the Skaara on course to invade the planet!"

They were face to face, inches away from each other. None of them was going to back down, and both had their own good reasons not to.

What the hell are we doing, thought Stephanie. She willed herself to break eye contact and step away, her hands raised to call a truce. "Agree to disagree, how about that?"

She waited for Lucy to relax, but the girl was still trembling, her fists clenched by her side. "I thought you were dead," she said. Her eyes were gleaming, on the verge of tears. "After the explosion, I checked all the news, I called all the hospitals in the area, but you disappeared. I thought you died, and I ... I thought I killed you."

Her voice cracked on the last word, and tears started flowing. Without a second thought, Stephanie's arms were around her, one hand on the back of her head, holding her against her shoulder. "It's okay," she whispered. "I'm okay. I'm here."

Stephanie expected resistance, but instead, Lucy's arms wrapped around her waist, the hug only growing tighter.

When she heard a noise from the stairs, Stephanie looked to the door to see Roxy's enquiring face looking in. She felt a moment of guilt at getting caught in that moment, a feeling she couldn't quite understand herself.

After a moment, it was Roxy who nodded in understanding, then slid away from the door.

With the privacy of the moment reestablished, Stephanie found herself holding Lucy closer. None of them would be ready to let go for a long while still.

Just as she walked through the door, Lucy heard Frank's voice coming from the living room. If her brother was back, then Matthew must have been home from work.

The next voice she heard, however, wasn't Matthew's. Lucy cringed at the idea of guests that late in the evening, and she heard next made her feel all the worse about it.

"We believe there is so much that we can do for you," a smooth masculine voice was saying, "just like there's a lot that you can do for us."

Lucy took her time in the hall to gather her thoughts. The meeting with Stephanie had shaken her up, and she wasn't sure she was ready for an Avis Carmen briefing just yet.

She took off her coat, then tried to shimmy her way past the living room door before anyone could catch her. Unfortunately, Matthew was sitting directly opposite the entrance. "Luce," he called. "Come here. You have to meet Oliver."

He stood up from the armchair to make the introductions, and Lucy wasn't quick enough at finding an excuse to slip away. She almost wanted to slap him as he kissed her on the cheek.

"Ah, Miss Campbell," the stranger said. He had stood up as well and was offering a hand to shake. "I've heard a lot about you. My name is Oliver Bennett. Most people call me Damien, though."

Lucy was suddenly conscious that, to anyone else in that room, she must have looked like a deer caught in the headlights. She forced herself to smile and relax her shoulders as she went to shake Bennett's hand. "I can't say I heard much about you, Mr Bennett."

"Damien, please."

Lucy forced a smile while shooting a piercing glare at Matthew. "To what do we owe the visit, *Damien*? Here to collect souls?"

"He's in charge of all the operations for Avis Carmen," interjected Matthew, clearly unhappy with her quip.

"He's here to recruit us," joined Frank from his spot on the sofa.

"I couldn't have put it better myself, Mr Campbell," intervened Damien. "You all were a great help already when you persuaded James Partridge to join in the effort to communicate with the Skaara. We believe there is more to come for you."

Lucy glanced at Frank's focused expression before looking at Damien again. His trimmed dark beard and steel blue eyes made him perfectly pleasant to look at, and he knew that. He exuded confidence. Something in the way he was standing made her think that nothing could happen in that room without him wanting so.

A sudden fear rushed through her mind. Victoria could have told someone about their encounter, and how Lucy had stolen her phone. The more she thought about it, the more Lucy realised she should have seen it coming. If that Demon Guy had been sent to look in on her, she wouldn't dare imagine what was in store for her.

Her hand was still resting in his, a gentle grip, yet firm enough to suggest she couldn't have retrieved her hand unless he let her. His eyes hadn't left hers for a second throughout the conversation.

She pulled her hand back, and he let her go. "Okay, Damien," she said, leaning against the armchair where Matthew had been sitting. "Shoot. What do you want us to do?"

He casually put his hands in his pockets and returned to sit on the sofa beside Frank. "I was just chatting to your brother about joining the Avis Carmen research team."

"I thought you were already doing a PhD," she said, turning to her brother.

"The two things are not exclusive, and the basic experiments are not too dissimilar," explained Frank. "Also, the Partridges are going to fund the research."

While Frank explained how Avis Carmen had managed to buy his services – Lucy could find no other way to put it – Matthew had taken his place in the armchair next to her, his arm softly wrapped around her waist. She felt surrounded. "Wow," she said without enthusiasm. "You're levelling up from brewing vodka, I see."

Frank tried to protest, "Luce—"

Lucy, however, wasn't going to give him time to counter. She turned to Damien. "Sounds like you won't be needing me, since you already picked the clever sibling."

He held her gaze. "You're the one who snuck the alien out of the laboratory once already," he said.

"Are you expecting an apology?"

She couldn't see where that was going, and that scared her.

"Oh no, I was actually impressed," he admitted. "That's what convinced me to offer you a job."

He had made no mention of Davis nor the beacon – not

yet, at least. The worst of it was that Matthew and Frank probably believed they had been blessed with his presence and bestowed sacred duties from Avis Carmen's Supreme Sorcerer, completely unaware of what was really going on behind their backs.

She faked a smile at him. "I'm not looking for a job at the moment."

Damien gave her an amused smile in return, and Lucy felt a shiver running up her spine. "You seem to have an affinity with the Skaara," he said. "A skill we could use in the field."

"I'm not sure I understand," she lied. The truth was that she wished she hadn't.

He leaned forward in his seat, elbows on his knees and hands joined as if in prayer. "Your skills are impressive, at least for someone who's never been trained. You are clever, and you are quick. You almost got the better of one of the best field agents SafeOp had to offer. I want you by my side to fight this alien menace."

The first mention of Davis. Lucy hoped no one had noticed when she flinched at hearing it. "She caught up with me," she said. "I didn't best anybody."

Damien's smile widened. "You're humble too."

Lucy ignored Frank's scoff at the remark, just as Damien did.

"I want you to start training with me as soon as possible," he continued. "Maybe we'll even get you a gun, as soon as we're sure you won't shoot any of us with it."

A light-hearted joke – or a subtle way of telling her he knew what she had been up to earlier that afternoon.

Her smile was frozen as she did her best not to let her nerves get the better of her. "It sounds exciting," she managed to say.

She doubted anyone had believed her, yet that barely mattered as Damien closed the argument with a slap of his thighs. "Fantastic," he decreed.

"Hey, hold on. I'm not sure about my sister getting a gun. Why don't I get one, then?" Frank protested from the corner. Lucy had almost forgotten it was supposed to be a group conversation.

Matthew quickly rebuked him, "Scientists don't get a gun, Frankie."

His arm was still around Lucy's waist, and he had started gently stroking her back. She felt like a puppy who had just aced a trick. She straightened up, moving away just enough for him to stop.

"What happens next, then?" she asked. "Are you going to whisk me away to a secret underground training camp? New face? New identity? Do I have to get a new haircut? Because I'm not sure I'm ready to go short."

She touched her ginger locks as if to demonstrate. Damien seemed amused at the joke, which made Lucy regret she had ever said it.

Matthew, however, was ready to take the fun out of it all. "You'll have to meet my parents before anything is agreed," he said.

Lucy couldn't have planned a worse nightmare in a decade of overthinking. "Say what now?"

"They're kind of in charge," he explained.

"Lady Partridge, a.k.a. Matthew's mum, is the patron of the Avis Carmen operation," specified Damien. "Nothing is decided without her consent."

The idea of running away in the middle of the night suddenly felt supremely attractive. She wondered if it was too late to hide in the boot of Davis's car. She wondered if Davis even had a car.

If I hid in the boot of her car, you'd bet that sexy muscle-bound bodyguard-not-bodyguard would find me and throw me in a ditch, she thought. The idea of that woman sharing the house with Davis had shaken her more than it should have.

"When am I going to meet the Lady of the Partridges, then?" she asked in an attempt to lock those thoughts away. She pivoted on her seat to better face Matthew.

He ignored her sarcasm. "We're driving down to the Hereford residence this weekend. Frankie as well."

She turned to Frank. "Does that mean I'm crashing your job interview?"

"Either that or I'm crashing your dinner with the in-laws," he replied good-humouredly.

Lucy smiled at that. It had been a while since they exchanged those kinds of jokes.

"You kids done?" interrupted Matthew.

Damien clearly had had enough as well. "Now that everything has been settled, I will take my leave. I will be in touch in due course, should the meeting with Lady Partridge be successful."

He made for the door, eager to leave before anyone could add anything else.

"Damien," called Lucy.

He stopped at the entrance, his hand raised to grab his coat. He barely turned his head as he called back. "Miss Campbell."

"Have you ever worked with Agent Davis?"

There was a long moment of silence. Lucy kept her gaze on him, yet she was aware of Matthew and Frank exchanging glances.

"Why do you ask?" he replied.

"I met her at the landing site right before the explosion," explained Lucy. "You say she was one of the best, but she did get herself blown up. That makes me wonder, is she really as good as you think she is?"

Damien turned to face her. There was a different gravity to his gaze as he processed the question. "The greatest mistake anyone could make is to underestimate what Davis is capable of. We worked together a long time ago, and I know first-hand how resourceful she can be. But I suppose you already knew that, didn't you?"

He left the question hanging in the room for just a moment, then he turned away and left the apartment.

Stephanie had been adamant she'd be travelling alone to Macclesfield. She was already putting Roxy at risk by staying at her house without having to drag her into her own quests.

Roxy had respectfully disagreed.

Stephanie intended to ignore that.

When she woke up on Thursday morning, winter darkness still covering the world outside, the keys to the car were nowhere to be found. That was, until Roxy appeared at the top of the stairs, dressed for the job and keys dangling from her outstretched hand. "It's over, Steph. I have the higher ground."

Stephanie rolled her eyes and shook her head, turning away before Roxy could catch a glimpse of her amused smile at the Star Wars joke.

After that, it was four long hours of driving from Bristol to Macclesfield in Roxy's old Yaris.

It wasn't until they drove onto the M5 that Roxy broke the silence. "Are you going to tell me about the girl?" she asked. Her tone was almost gentle.

"It's not what you think," replied Stephanie, immediately realising how defensive that must have sounded. "It's nothing you should worry about," she added, a weak attempt at recovery.

"Oh, I don't know about that," countered Roxy, her tone still level. "Not only did I come back home to find you moved back in. Shortly after that, I have your new girlfriend knocking on the door, and now I'm driving you to a secret mission in fucking Macclesfield, of all useless places. All the while" – she raised a hand to stop Stephanie from interrupting – "all the while, I'm told you're supposed to be dead, blown up by an exploding spaceship. Did I miss anything?"

Stephanie exhaled. "The alien," she said.

"Oh right, I almost forgot you got mind-controlled by E.T. and that we're about to be invaded. Now, would you stop being a dick and tell me about the girl?"

"Of all the things you listed, you want to know about Lucy?" asked Stephanie. The hint of guilt she had felt the day before had rekindled in her chest.

"Listen, babe," said Roxy, and Stephanie braced for what would come next. "I love you, you know that, and I trust you know how to do your job, however stupid this whole mess sounds. But people? Not your forte. You bring that girl into my home, I want to know about her. Does that seem fair?"

"You're reading too much into this. She's just a civilian who got caught in the middle," explained Stephanie. She was speaking the truth, yet the words felt stale in her mouth.

Roxy was quiet for a while. She gripped the steering wheel as if holding herself back rather than holding the car on course. "Steph," she said eventually. "I've seen the way you looked at her. The same way you used to look at me. And the way you held on to her? Hon, if you got feelings, I have to know you're at least aware of your bias."

"I don't *have* feelings. She's no one. A contingency."

"Way back when, people would say the same thing about

you."

Stephanie bit her lip. She hated how Roxy's words made sense, yet she couldn't allow herself to feel that way. She crossed her arms on her chest and turned to the window.

None of them said anything for the rest of the journey. Roxy turned on the radio to fill the silence, leaving them to listen to BBC Radio 6's choice of music.

The clock on the dashboard showed the time as 10:17 when they arrived in Macclesfield.

Roxy parked the car by the side of the road and turned off the engine. The radio fell silent, adding to the silence. "Do you have everything you need?" she asked.

Stephanie stared dead ahead towards the line of houses that included James Partridge's semi-detached. "I'm all set," she said. "Are you?"

Roxy nodded. "I'll be back in an hour to pick you up."

"The sooner the better. I might be leaving in a hurry."

Without waiting for an answer, Stephanie got out of the car and set off to walk the last few hundred yards to James Partridge's residence. As she walked slowly along the sidewalk, she felt the sting of the morning air on her cheeks. A pale sun was out, yet she knew it wasn't going to make much of a difference.

It was an uninterrupted row of semi-detached houses on her right, the civic numbers building up as she moved closer to her destination. She stopped a couple of doorsteps away and glanced ahead.

She could see a car parked on the driveway of Mr Partridge's house. From where she was standing, however, she couldn't see if anyone was guarding the front door, although she fully expected that to be so.

After Lucy's visit, there couldn't be any doubt Avis Carmen was keeping an eye on her, and Stephanie knew Roxy's presence was the only thing between her and a forced retreat at Victoria Evans' country house once again. Stephanie wondered how long it'd take for Millican to reach out and recruit her ex-partner. It was possible they were just waiting for the right moment – Stephanie's arrest for breaking and entering a civilian's house, for example.

She had to assume the surveillance detail had been alerted of her arrival.

Stephanie paused on the sidewalk. She had to talk to James Partridge and understand more about the Avis Carmen operation and the beacon Lucy had given her. What she didn't need was niggling self-doubt and doom-self-talk.

In her pocket, she felt the shape of the beacon against her hand.

I can do this.

She took a deep breath in, closed her eyes, and exhaled slowly, then resumed her walk, past Mr Partridge's house and all the way to the end of the road. From there, she turned right and into the field, circling the residential properties and making her way back on the other side, keeping close enough to the fences to avoid being too noticeable to anyone looking out the windows.

Stephanie counted the houses until she reached Mr Partridge's. Much like all the others, his garden was surrounded by a six-foot tall fence. Not as easy as jumping across a hedge, and possibly more than she could manage after three months of inactivity while recovering from the explosion.

Behind her, the rail tracks and the sound of a train in the distance. She inspected the fence, finding one of the corners had got loose and offered a small space she could fit through. The best thing about it was the garden furniture placed right in front of it, offering perfect cover from the backdoor.

She pushed her head through to survey the garden. She had expected at least one guard to be stationed there, yet the space was empty.

This is too easy, she thought.

Stephanie slid through the opening, keeping herself out of sight. The train came rushing a few hundred yards away as she silently made her way to a blind spot to the side of the house.

She still wasn't sure how many agents were inside. It could have been two, or it could have been ten, all hidden in the living room, ready for her surprise welcome party.

The small rocks peppering the flowerbed gave her an idea. She picked up the smallest one, as big as her fingernail, and threw it at the back door. The impact was loud enough to alert one of the neighbourhood's dogs, who promptly started barking from a few gardens away.

Stephanie waited.

A few seconds later, the backdoor opened, and a large figure in a SafeOp uniform stepped out into the garden. He had a gun clipped to his belt and a Taser in his hand.

The silent choice that doesn't get you arrested for murder. Clever.

He was never going to have a chance to use it, though, as Stephanie sneaked up behind him and trapped him in a rear-neck choke before he could utter a word. Still, he raised the Taser, and she felt the jolt of current coursing through her arm. She held on tight, her muscles contracting despite herself, until the guard quietly folded to the ground, his arm falling limp to his side.

Her right arm still twitching, Stephanie dragged the guard's body to the side and checked his pulse – still alive. She sighed in relief.

Next, she checked his gear. The gun was a tranquiliser and was equipped with a silencer. She took it off him and checked the cartridge – full load.

"Sorry, buddy," she murmured, firing one in his right arm. She then clipped the gun to her own belt. With that and the Taser gun added to her arsenal, the day ahead already looked easier.

The garden door was still open, and no one had shown up to check what had just happened. Stephanie readied the Taser gun and surveyed the space inside.

The living room appeared empty.

Silently, she stepped past the sofa, dodging the coffee table, then through the door and along the hall to the small kitchen. Still not a soul in sight.

Stephanie was starting to wonder if Lucy hadn't sent her on a wild-goose chase when she heard floorboards creaking upstairs, then a voice saying, "We got company. You stay there. I'll take care of it."

She knew what was going to happen next.

The stairs leading up to the first floor started right in front of the kitchen door. Stephanie hid behind the fridge, making sure she had a good visual of the doorway while remaining behind cover.

For long seconds, she listened for footsteps, while the only sound she could hear was her heart beating. She silently exhaled, then checked her grip on the Taser gun.

A creaking sound came from the stairs as the agent crept downward. Then silence.

Stephanie kept still.

If both agents were ex-SafeOp men, she knew how they were trained, which worked to her advantage. The best thing to do was to wait and keep still.

There was movement on the stairs once again. Stephanie could picture the agent holding the gun at his shoulder, ready to shoot anyone he could spot in the kitchen while he covered the last steps.

Once on the ground floor, he would check the kitchen first before heading to the living room. Stephanie would have one chance, and she would have to be fast. First, though, she had to wait.

She pictured him taking his time, slicing the pie to check for any intruder in the kitchen while also keeping an eye on the living room directly on his left. It was what she would've done, just like they had been trained to do. However careful he managed to be, his attention was divided, which would give Stephanie an opening.

She chanced a glance at the room. The agent was almost fully exposed in the doorway. He hadn't spotted her and was increasingly preoccupied with checking his left flank.

Stephanie didn't wait for a better chance. She stretched her arm out and pulled the trigger of the Taser gun. A shot was fired, which hit the cupboard ahead.

Releasing the trigger, Stephanie dropped the Taser and drew the gun. When she glanced at the room, however, the twitching shape of a SafeOp agent was sprawled on the floor.

She took his gun – a tranquiliser equipped with a silencer, just like his colleague – and shot him in the arm.

"Nighty-night," she heard herself whisper before slipping past him and heading up the stairs.

Stepping on the landing, she found three doors. Two gave

onto empty bedrooms. The third door was closed. Mr Partridge must have been in there.

Stephanie readied the Taser and approached the door.

She was prepared to turn the handle when a man's shaky voice came from the other side. "Whoever you are, I must warn you! I am armed!"

It appeared Mr Partridge had been left to fend for himself. "I'm not here to hurt you, Mr Partridge," she said. "I only want to talk."

"You can talk to my sister, if you manage to book an audience."

"That's on my list, but I'd like to talk to you first," she replied firmly. "I'm coming in," she added when he didn't reply.

She holstered the Taser gun, turned the handle, and pushed the door open, keeping the wooden frame between herself and the armed Mr Partridge.

When nothing happened at the wide-open door, she slowly came out of hiding, her empty hands raised above her head.

In front of her, a tall white-haired man was standing in the corner, a lamp held over his head, threatening to either throw it or bash her head with it. The man didn't look like he knew which one he was going to choose. Before he could make up his mind, Stephanie spoke, "My name is Stephanie Davis. I came to get you out of here."

"Have you got Ellie with you?" he asked, almost defiant.

"No," she admitted, trying to quickly put the pieces together before hazarding a guess. "She's your daughter, isn't she?"

Even though her guess was right, it wasn't enough to convince Partridge. "You have no idea what's going on, do you?"

Stephanie wished he'd put the lamp down so they could start telling tales. "I know that your sister is leading something called Avis Carmen and that she needs you to build a communication system. I suppose they took your daughter hostage to force your cooperation."

"I'm not building anything for them," he countered.

"That's good to hear," replied Stephanie. "My guess is that they can't communicate with the Skaara warship without your help, and if they can't trick them into a parlay, our space friends will land on Earth with guns a-blazing to avenge the scout that your sister is keeping prisoner in a lab somewhere. How am I doing?"

Partridge was still staring her down, but he hadn't thrown the lamp yet. Stephanie counted that as a small victory.

She continued, "If you're not building anything, it must be because the equipment is already there, maybe from the days you first talked to the Skaara. They can't use it, though, because you took the instruction manual with you when you left."

A short pause as Partridge lowered his gaze.

Stephanie's shoulders had started to get sore with the effort of keeping her arms up. She pressed on, "Fun thing about all of that is, if they don't know how to use it, they won't know that you're doing it wrong on purpose. You're planning to break the communication and let the Skaara kill them on landing, aren't you? Smart plan, I'll admit. What you haven't considered, though, is that the Skaara will not stop after killing your sister's acolytes."

Stephanie took a breath. "Now, would you please put that lamp down so we can talk about how to fix this?"

Partridge exhaled and lowered the lamp. "Ellie is my daughter. You've got that right."

Stephanie lowered her arms, then waited. It looked as if there was a lot bearing on him, and a lot he wanted to share. However, when he sat back on his chair, he turned to his desk and said, "You have to leave."

"Not until we talk, and not without you."

"They'll hurt Ellie as soon as they realise you've been here, and if I leave, they'll kill her," he explained, his head lowered and his hands gripping the chair's armrests. "You have to leave."

The same organisation bent on protecting the Earth clearly didn't think much of hurting those who inhabited it. What else was new? "I will," conceded Stephanie. "Once you tell me what I need to know."

From the pocket, she produced the small black beacon that Lucy had entrusted her with. She handed it over to Partridge. "I believe you know what this is. Do you know how it works?"

The beacon was still pulsing, same as it had been the previous day. It hadn't slowed down, nor it had sped up. When Partridge saw it, his eyes went wide. "It's activated."

He reached out a hand to receive it, and Stephanie let him examine the device under his desk lamp, wondering what he was hoping to see through all that blackness.

"Do you know what it's signalling?" she asked after a few moments of silence.

It didn't look like he heard the question. "This is the homing beacon that directed the first Skaara spaceship."

"Gwyn's spaceship?" interjected Stephanie. "That already landed. What's the point of activating it again?"

Partridge glanced sideways at her, as if she had just made the most pointless comment. "A homing beacon can direct many ships. You say my sister is expecting a warship. I say this is proof that something is coming our way. Whether it's a warship or a hunting party, I'll let you make your guess."

"Do you think the Skaara are moving to invade?" she asked.

"An invasion was never in their plans," he explained. "The Skaara are a peaceful species, unless provoked."

Stephanie scoffed. "Are you sure about that? They never seemed very peaceful to me."

"Their planet was dying, so they fled. They came to Earth to find a new home to share with the existing species," he explained. "That's what they told me, at least, when I picked up their message at the beginning." He paused, as if considering his next words. "If you care for my opinion, I'd doubt they even have weapons on that ship of theirs. If they had meant to use force, they would have already."

Stephanie could see the logic of his reasoning, and part of her even agreed with it.

While he talked, Partridge turned the beacon in his hands, running his fingers along invisible lines on the surface. "It's a fascinating technology. Unfortunately, beacons are remotely activated. No way to turn it off."

A grimace crossed Stephanie's face. "I thought you'd say that. Any idea what to do with it?"

He swivelled his chair around to look at her. "Yes. Take this as far away from here and Avis Carmen as you can."

That was not helpful. "I got that far on my own, thank you." She was getting tired of his dismissive tone, as if she wasn't aware of the stakes of the game. "How does it work?"

"Very well," he said with a sigh. "The beacon is part of a larger kit that the Skaara sent to Earth around six years ago. It came with an inbuilt translator of sorts, and something like an instruction manual."

"What's the equivalent of an instruction manual? Does your sister have it?" asked Stephanie.

"It's a codex that allows you to interpret the Skaara signals," he explained. "Their language consists of electrical impulses, ion currents, light beams – anything that behaves like a particle wave, they can use and perceive."

Never a big fan of particle physics, Partridge's explanation oddly made sense to Stephanie. "Is that how they control humans, by sending signals to their brains?"

Partridge cocked his head, taken aback by the question. "They can do that?"

Stephanie chuckled. "You don't know everything about the space crawlers, it seems," she commented with a smirk. "Why did you leave your family after contacting the Skaara?" she asked, bringing the conversation back on track.

A look of distrust crossed Partridge's face. "Who told you that?"

"We have a friend in common," replied Stephanie. "I believe you met Lucy. She was one of those who found the Skaara's spaceship in the Forest of Dean."

Partridge nodded, as if that name was enough to guarantee Stephanie was on the right side. "My sister had plans. I didn't like them."

"What plans?"

He shrugged. "Profit, of course. She saw technology that outclassed anything we have on Earth. If she could take control of it, she'd be ruling the world, which is basically what Avis Carmen is there for."

Stephanie exhaled. Naturally, it all came down to money and greed. With humans, it was rarely a different story.

An ugly picture had started to take shape in her mind. "She thinks she can overpower them. Do you know how she plans to do that?"

"No idea," he confessed. "If she found a way to block the Skaara mind-control, that might be her way to neutralise them altogether."

Neutralise. A soft word to describe what Avis Carmen was likely planning to do. Stephanie shook her head. "What I don't understand is, if she wants their technology, why not just trade with them? Why aim straight for mass murder?"

Partridge raised her a wistful gaze. "Skaara are not interested in resources. They want us."

She couldn't have heard that right. "Beg your pardon?"

"The Skaara cannot live independently. Not for long, at least. They need a host. A willing one, preferably. Although you mentioned they can control people, so I suppose an unwilling one would do just as well."

Stephanie's mind went back to her own experience with Gwyn. She almost felt her shape clinging to her shoulders once again, drawing blood as she did so. She had thought that deliberate, an act of violence, even. Stephanie was beginning to see the other side of that story.

"I suppose bringing this to the authorities is not an option," she said to no particular purpose. She had already dismissed that as a viable option.

Partridge shared that opinion. "She already convinced her friends in parliament that she can outwit a whole alien species and get away with a prize."

"She's delusional."

"Maybe," he conceded. "She's also in charge."

Pushing herself off the desk, Stephanie started pacing the room. There had to be a way out of that. She just needed to find the right pressure point. The right plan. "Is there any way to contact the Skaara ship before your sister does?"

He exhaled. "I'm afraid not. She has the only working apparatus. It's the one I built before she threw me out."

"I thought you were the one who left?"

Partridge dismissed the comment. "Semantics." He then raised the beacon as if to give it back. "There's one bit of good news I can give you, though."

Stephanie stopped her pacing, arms crossed on her chest. "Please."

"The equipment is useless without the transmitter."

It wasn't much, but it gave her at least an opening. "You mean she can't contact the Skaara's ship and arrange the landing without the beacon."

"More or less," said Partridge. "The Skaara will still follow the homing signal and make their way to Earth, but my sister won't be able to coordinate any of it."

Not as good an option as Stephanie had hoped for. "That's not a smart plan, I told you."

"Anything that prevents my sister from taking over the world is a good plan," he replied.

It was easy to understand Partridge's point of view, yet that didn't make the prospect of a Skaara-controlled army any more acceptable. "Do you know where they're keeping the comms equipment?" she asked.

"It used to be in the Highlands, but they moved everything to Herefordshire when the Duckworth offered their summer house to accommodate the Avis Carmen operations."

Stephanie nodded, then reached out a hand to take the beacon from him. "Thank you. That was all very helpful."

"Maybe," he said with a shrug. "If you're going to try to stop them, there's one more thing you should probably know."

"Go on."

"Sym-Bio-Tech's board of directors has acquired a new member as of last month," he said. "Anthony Cavell has just been appointed. I can't be sure, but if I had a space alien I wanted to study, I'd make sure to have a laboratory available to do that."

That was the most solid lead Stephanie had been given since leaving Victoria's house. Not that she was looking forward to a reunion with the Skaara, but she needed Gwyn's cooperation to prevent the slaughter of the spaceship crew due for landing.

"Listen, Stephanie," said Partridge, breaking the momentary silence as well as Stephanie's train of thought, "Whatever you're planning to do, the first thing should be to get out of here before someone sees you."

Stephanie placed the beacon securely in her pocket once again. "The boys downstairs are going to be asleep for a few hours. You should have some peace and quiet until then. What are you going to tell them?"

"That you came to ask about Avis Carmen and that I told you to go talk to my sister," he said.

"The truth, then," she commented with half a smile.

Partridge shrugged. "The only thing you could have taken away is me, and I'm still here."

Stephanie nodded. "I'll find a way to get you out of this."

He swivelled his chair and went back to his work. "Just go get my sister."

- IX -

The local train rattled past as Lucy walked to the door.

The plan had been to visit Sophie. Her house, however, was only a few minutes' walk from where Davis was staying, and Lucy's feet had carried her there before she realised what she was doing.

It had been two days since she had been there last. Two days since Damien Bennett had shown up at the flat. Two days since Matthew had started planning a visit to his parents to seal their fate into Avis Carmen.

She felt her stomach crunch in anticipation. It was even possible Davis wasn't going to be there. Not if she had moved on to the next item on her to-do list. Or if something had gone wrong at Uncle Jim's.

The doorbell rang inside the house when she pressed it.

As she waited, Lucy clenched her fists in her pockets while she glanced at the late afternoon darkness around her. She wondered if Damien had someone watching her at that very moment.

I have to tell her about this, she thought.

It felt obvious how Davis had to know about Damien and the risk he presented. Even so, Lucy hated how important that woman had become in her life. She hated the power Davis seemed to have over her.

When the door finally opened, Lucy had to refrain from shooting through the doorway and inside the hall. "Hey," she managed, almost out of breath.

Roxy looked perplexed at her presence there. "Hey," she responded, moving aside to let her in.

Inside the hall, there was a moment of hesitation. Lucy was about to say something when Roxy asked, "Did the Cavell send you?"

"No," replied Lucy. The distrust in Roxy's voice hurt more than she expected. "Matthew doesn't know about any of this."

Hands on her hips, Roxy raised her eyebrows at the comment. "Sure he doesn't. And I suppose his parents and the whole Avis Carmen also don't know why you're visiting Steph's safe house twice in a week. It seems to me you've been sent here. Or are you going to tell me you're just doing it for love?"

The woman's words felt like a stab to her chest. They were still standing in the hall. For all Lucy knew, Davis wasn't even home. She stumbled back towards the door. "I see I'm not welcome here. I better go."

Her hand was on the latch when Davis's voice stopped her. "Lucy, wait, please. I'm sorry. Roxy's just... well, she's being Roxy, I suppose."

Lucy turned in time to see Roxy roll her eyes. "Oh, yeah, sure. Just being me." She turned and started up the stairs. "I'll be upstairs if anyone needs me. Just there, being Roxy again." She exhaled on the last step. "I just hope you know what you're doing, Steph."

It was only when Roxy disappeared up the stairs that Davis said, "Come in. I'll make some coffee."

She walked on into the kitchen for a conciliatory cup of coffee.

"How was Uncle Jim?" she asked. She took a seat at the table while Davis busied herself with the coffees.

"Your boyfriend convinced him to cooperate in the Avis Carmen operation by threatening his daughter," she said.

Lucy really wished everyone would stop calling Matthew her boyfriend.

"Is he doing okay, though?" she asked again.

"He's stuck in a corner, but he's holding on."

"Any chance of getting him out of there?" she asked, although she already knew the answer. If there was, Uncle Jim would've been sitting at the table with them.

"It's better he stays where he is, for now," said Davis, reaching for the sugar bowl. "One sugar?"

"One and a half," corrected Lucy. She watched Davis add the sugar and stir the coffees. Only when Davis finally sat at the table with her did Lucy realise she had been staring. She diverted her gaze, then asked, "What about the beacon? Did you figure out what it's for?"

"I did," replied Davis.

Lucy expected her to continue, however she only lifted the mug of coffee to her lips and gently blew the steam away.

So that's how it's going to be, she thought. With Roxy as her sidekick, Davis had no need for one more nosy troublemaker around her – or at least that's what Lucy imagined Davis was thinking. She could almost picture them talking about what a nuisance she was, sitting on the sofa in the evening, sipping tea, or wine, or whatever it was that this Roxy drank.

"You do realise that, if I wasn't on your side, I could've had the Avis Carmen's agents storming this place already?" she said, trying and failing to hide the annoyance.

"Not true," replied Davis, unfazed by Lucy's impetus. "They

know where I am, and they know Roxy's here. If they wanted to get to me, they'd bring her on board first."

"How do you know they haven't already?"

"Roxy and I have been through a lot together. She'd tell me if she'd been approached. Besides, I expect they'll want to know what I'm up to before making a move."

"Is that so?" snapped back Lucy, her frustration rising against Davis's unwavering composure. "Just remind me, what *would* you be up to if I hadn't told you about Uncle Jim? And what would you have talked to him about if I hadn't given you the beacon? Or the flash drive?"

Davis's lips parted as if to answer, but she spoke no word. She lowered her gaze instead, keeping her silence. To Lucy, she looked like a parent waiting for their child to run out of steam during a tantrum. It was more than Lucy could take.

"You're still full of shit, like you were before you died," she snapped as she jumped up from the chair and stomped to the window, her arms tensed and crossed on her chest to hide her clenching fists. She could feel her nails digging into her palms. She felt the pain, and she clenched faster.

"It's not about you," said Davis eventually.

Lucy frowned yet resisted the urge to turn around, not wanting Davis to see her reaction. "Of course not. Because it's all about you, isn't it?" she barked instead.

"I'm just trying to keep you safe."

Lucy wasn't going to have any of that. "Are you listening to yourself?" she snapped, turning to face her this time. "You want me to be safe? I live with the next in line to the throne of this cultish Avis Carmen thing. My brother is on their payroll and about to join their research team. Oh, and let's not forget about the ship full of brain leeches about to land in our backyard.

You think you can keep me safe? I have Avis Carmen's agents coming over for dinner on a regular basis! Guess who's the delusional one right now."

Davis, however, wasn't going to back down either. She stood up from her chair to bring herself at eye level with Lucy, who had to make an effort not to step backwards at the strength of her quiet resoluteness.

"You need to stay away from here," she said. Her tone was still calm, yet the tension was building in the room. "I am grateful for your help, but if they find out you come here on a regular basis, I can't keep you safe. I'm asking you to step away and let me take care of this."

The air was crackling around them.

Lucy was finding it hard not to scream at Davis. "You can't just lone-wolf this whole thing."

"I'm not."

"Bullshit," said Lucy with a scoff. Her temper was getting the better of her. Before she could stop herself, words were rushing out of her mouth. "Then I should probably tell you, Matthew's taking me to meet the in-laws this weekend. If it's a wedding proposal or a job interview, I still haven't figured it out. You want me to step away? No chance they'll even let me."

Davis blinked in surprise at the waterfall of information. "There's a lot going on, I see," she said, then looked away. "Things are getting pretty serious with you two."

At the sight of Davis's reaction, Lucy regretted her choice of words while all her steaming rage subsided. "It's not a marriage proposal. I don't know why I said that," she said, trying to recover. "It's a job interview. A big-shot guy came to visit the other day, after I left here. He recruited both me and Frankie."

Davis looked up in alarm. "Does the big shot have a name?"

There was urgency in her tone, and Lucy couldn't help feeling a spark of vindication at the attention Davis was finally giving her. "It's your old friend Bennett. At least he said you worked together in the past."

Lucy wasn't sure what reaction she expected from her — maybe some stern instruction to stay out of trouble and leave the Damien Guy to her. Davis, however, just nodded, then sat down at the table again, hands around her mug of coffee. She took a sip, wrinkles on her forehead the only detail to betray her worry.

Lucy wasn't sure what that meant. "Aren't you going to say anything?"

"Where are you going to meet them?" asked Davis. "The in-laws, I mean."

"Herefordshire," replied Lucy, puzzled as to how she'd be still thinking about that.

"Did they mention anyone else who'd be present? Maybe by the name Millican?"

Lucy shook her head. "Doesn't ring a bell, no."

Davis nodded again, then resumed her deep thinking. Lucy sat back down at the table with her. "You're cooking up a spymaster plan, aren't you?"

Another sip of her coffee, and Davis reached out a hand as if she hadn't even heard the question. "Give me your phone."

"You're doing it wrong," replied Lucy, unable to stop herself. "You're supposed to ask for my number, not the whole phone."

With a jiggle of her fingers, Davis renewed the request. Lucy took it from her pocket, unlocked it, and handed it over. "What do you need with it?"

A few seconds and some tapping later, Davis gave it back. "If you hear anything I should know, or if you spot trouble, send a message to Amelie," she explained. "A simple message, the old-fashioned way."

"Could you be any less specific? What am I supposed to tell Amelie?" asked Lucy, more puzzled than ever. "And who's Amelie anyway?"

Davis stretched behind her to pick up an old Nokia phone from the kitchen counter. "Amelie," she said as if demonstrating. "I could hardly register a SIM card with my real name, now, could I?".

"Wow," commented Lucy, staring at the technological relic. "All the way from 2004."

Half a smile appeared on Davis's face. Lucy allowed herself a gulp of coffee to celebrate cracking the icy surface. She relaxed in her chair, the initial tension entirely dispelled. She didn't want to believe they were finally on level terms, but having a way to contact Davis in times of need was definitely a step in that direction.

Maybe now she'll even tell me what she's up to, she mused. "What are you going to do while I'm sipping tea with the enemy?"

"I think I know where they're keeping Gwyn," explained Davis. "I'm going to get her out, before it's too late."

Lucy's mug landed heavily on the table, coffee spilling over the side at the impetus. "No. You don't mean that."

There was a frown of confusion on Davis's face. "Weren't you the one advocating freeing all Skaara from imprisonment?"

"Yes, but I didn't mean you have to do it yourself! After what she did to you last time? And what you did to her?"

"I didn't do anything to her," specified Davis quickly.

"You blew up her spaceship and all of her pods," insisted Lucy. "She might have taken it personally."

Davis sighed. "You have to trust me. I know what I'm doing."

"Do you?" snapped Lucy. "You're so worried about protecting me, but what about you? What if she tries to kill you this time? Or hijacks your brain again and starts driving you around like her personal human carrier? She's done it to you once. What if she does it again?"

The smile spreading on Davis's lips softened up her features. "You're worried about me."

Lucy hadn't expected that. She averted her gaze. "Somebody has to," she mumbled.

"I know what I'm doing," repeated Davis. Her hand had gone to rest on Lucy's arm, as if to placate her somehow. "Trust me."

Feeling the contact of Davis's hand, Lucy didn't know what to say. For someone as deeply distrustful as she was, every part of her wanted to trust the woman in front of her. "You know what she's capable of," she said, a half-hearted attempt.

"Lucy."

That was enough. Lucy knew it was a lost fight. "Tell Gwyn I said hi, I guess."

* * *

She was supposed to arrive at Sophie's before six, yet the short visit to Davis had needed a longer walk to clear her head. Even so, when her friend opened the door, she was sure her face still betrayed the apprehension she felt after her conversation with Davis.

Her head still haunted by visions of the upcoming reunion between human, Davis, and Skaara, Gwyn, Lucy left Sophie to take care of the drinks – a hot infusion for her, since she looked like she needed to relax, her friend had said.

A few minutes later, Lucy sat on the same sofa bed she had slept on for three years, her legs gathered to her chest, ankles crossed. She was holding a steaming mug of something that smelled of apples and spice.

"You're taking your time with the redecoration," she commented.

Sophie was sitting on the opposite corner of the sofa, crossed-legged, her mug in her lap. "Did you expect me to turn it into a gym the moment you left?"

Lucy shook her head. "A gym? No. A pottery studio? Maybe."

Sophie chuckled. "The thought did cross my mind." She cocked her head, then asked, "Are you going to tell me what's wrong?"

Lucy tapped her fingers on the side of the mug. She couldn't find the right words to start. It didn't help that there was a whole side of the story she couldn't share with Sophie if she wanted to.

"How's Frank doing?" asked Sophie. Lucy knew it was her way to slowly inch towards the heart of the problem. She had done it many times.

"He's okay. He keeps himself busy at uni, and Matthew's family offered him a job, so yeah, he's doing okay." She stopped herself before the words *Avis Carmen* would slip out.

It was still enough for Sophie's ears to perk up. "I thought Frank was all about his PhD."

"He was. He is." She had no idea how to explain any of it. "Matthew's family runs this organisation, and they offered him to fund his research if he joins them. It's a big opportunity, apparently."

Sophie raised an eyebrow. "Apparently?"

"He seems excited about it."

"And you?"

Lucy exhaled. "I don't know," she said, then more confidently. "No, I'm not. I don't like it, actually."

Sophie nodded and waited, a kind and soft look on her face.

There was a knot at the mouth of Lucy's stomach and a haze over her eyes. Staring at the rivulets of steam rising from her mug, she couldn't remember the last time she hadn't felt that exhausted. She thought meeting Davis would turn things around, but it had only gone so far.

She glanced up at Sophie. "Do you remember that agent that died in the explosion? I told you about her."

"You're still thinking about that?" asked Sophie. Her tone sounded worried.

"Hard not to," replied Lucy, a finger tracing the rim of her mug as she took her time with the answer. "She's alive."

To Sophie's credit, she hid her shock admirably well. "What?" she managed.

"Oh, you know, super spy skills and all that," said Lucy, waving the subject away. "She survived the explosion and found Frank, who naturally ran home to tell me."

An expectant stare was all the answer Sophie gave her, so Lucy continued. "Well, I went looking for her," she admitted, then, as Sophie started her protest, she added, "I know it was stupid, but I had to see her, so I went to visit, and there she was. Alive." She took a deep breath and found herself smiling at the thought for the first time. "I didn't kill her."

Sophie gave her a warm smile in response. "No, you didn't."

Lucy revelled in that moment, only to remember how Davis's next quest was just as likely to kill her as the explosion she barely survived. When she looked back at Sophie, her smile lingered, a dash of mischief around its corners. "What?" asked

Lucy.

"Are you going to tell me what happened when you went to visit her?"

Despite her efforts, Lucy couldn't stop herself from grinning at the question. "We talked, then I left. Both times, because, well, I went twice," she admitted, then glanced at Sophie's reaction and rushed to add, "Nothing happened, stop smiling like that!"

Sophie exhaled but did not stop smiling. "Oh, Lucy," she said. "Stop that."

"Just tell me, do you want me to prepare the room for you, or are you moving in with the secret agent right away?"

Lucy chuckled at that. "You're an idiot."

"Maybe, but I don't hear you saying I'm wrong."

That was because Sophie was right, no matter how unlikely it was that anything good would result from those feelings.

"Matthew is taking me to meet his parents, so don't throw away your bridesmaid dress just yet," she joked.

There was shock on Sophie's face. They both knew how the Cavells had always looked down on Lucy. Running away from home at sixteen wasn't on the list of desirable attributes in a future daughter-in-law. "Is he, like, proposing?"

"More like a job interview, I think," explained Lucy. "They got Frankie roped in already, why not get the wayward sister as well?"

"Are you sure it's the right thing to do?"

Lucy couldn't answer that question. Her reasons for going through with it had nothing to do with her feelings for Matthew. "Are they still showing *Friends* on Netflix?" she asked, attempting to change the subject.

Sophie, however, wasn't buying it. "You're not going to make it go away just by not talking about it, no matter how much of it is sensitive secret service stuff," she insisted.

Lucy nodded. "Thank you, Soph."

"That's okay. I got you, Luce."

- X -

It took almost two hours to finally reach the Herefordshire laboratories of Sym-Bio-Tech. For once, Stephanie hadn't even tried to persuade Roxy to stay home.

"Are you sure you're ready to reunite with the little fella?" asked Roxy, the Welsh woodland rushing past them.

Stephanie's wistful gaze was resting on the road ahead. "I have to. There's no other way."

"I could do it, you know."

"You go in there instead of me, and you put a target on both of our heads," retorted Stephanie. "The Skaara is not the danger here. We talked about this."

"Millican doesn't scare me," replied Roxy. "I'm worried about you."

Stephanie exhaled. "I know."

The heavy silence that followed lasted for a long time, filled only with the rumbling of the local Welsh radio station.

Finding Gwyn and breaking her out was going to be a challenge, no less because she couldn't be sure how the Skaara would react to her presence. In all honesty, Stephanie wasn't too sure how she was going to react at seeing the Skaara again either.

It wasn't something she liked to dwell on. She could still feel the weight of the Skaara on her shoulders whenever she closed her eyes, remembering the long hours she had spent trapped in a corner of her own mind while Gwyn commandeered the rest of her body.

She shrugged the memory off and locked it away.

When Roxy finally parked the yellow Toyota under the cover of a large oak tree, it was only minutes before eight o'clock in the morning. The sun was just about showing on the hazy horizon.

"We're early," said Stephanie.

"You're the one who wanted to leave early," replied Roxy.

Stephanie pushed the seat as far back as it would go and took out Roxy's laptop to revise the plan.

"It's not like you to be this nervous," commented Roxy, watching her browsing through plans of the facility and intel about Sym-Bio-Tech.

"I'm not," lied Stephanie. She wouldn't admit it to Roxy, but she had a bad feeling about it. There was no logical reason to, as she had the element of surprise on her side. She had studied the facility, had brought all the tools she needed, and had the experience and training that were going to see her through. Even so, the feeling kept nagging at her.

Roxy sank back into her seat. "Chances of him being here are slim," she said. She was talking about Bennett, the ghost of Stephanie's Christmas Past.

"You don't know that," replied Stephanie. "Shall we go through the plan again?"

They knew a metallic fencing surrounded the building to prevent unauthorised access. The premises were likely covered by cameras, and Stephanie couldn't exclude motion sensors on the whole perimeter as well.

"You've got the interference pen to neutralise the cameras, but that only works from a range of five metres," she explained. "Do you think you can get close enough without being spotted?"

Stephanie peered at the view before bringing up a satellite image of the valley. "Cover shouldn't be a problem," she said, pointing at the screen in correspondence with a couple of structures on the edge of the fenced area. "The problem will be getting there. I expected more bushes on the way down."

"I really don't think there'll be many science geeks looking wistfully out the window in our direction," mused Roxy.

Stephanie sneered. "Solid strategy, yours. Where did you learn it from, *Positive Thinking for Spies*?"

Roxy rolled her eyes. "I packed the camo jacket, you dummy. You'll be fine."

Despite herself, Stephanie smiled. Roxy's sense of humour had a calming effect on her – it always had. It made her think that all would be fine, even if her gut feeling was certain of the opposite.

Once the outside cameras were disabled, Stephanie would enter the facility. Inside, she expected each door to have a magnetic lock requiring a pass, which she'd have to borrow from one of the employees.

"How many rounds did you get in Macclesfield?" asked Roxy.

"Two. I should have enough tranquiliser to put the whole business to sleep," replied Stephanie. She unholstered the gun and checked it, then slipped it back in its place. From another compartment, she extracted the Taser. "And then I have this."

"I hate those things," said Roxy with a grimace.

Stephanie smirked. "Trauma reaction much?"

"You sneaked up on me."

"I had a bet to win."

Silence held for a moment before both Stephanie and Roxy burst out laughing, glancing at each other as if not quite believing those memories were still there – as if quite not believing that the past was still part of them.

As the laughter slowly waned, Stephanie wiped a tear from her eye. A glance at the clock on the dashboard told her it was time to go. "Two hours," she said. If I'm not back, leave."

"You know I won't," replied Roxy.

"I know, but you should."

Leaving the laptop in the passenger seat, Stephanie stepped out of the car. There was an invigorating freshness to the morning air. For once, she wasn't feeling the cold so much.

She took her backpack and Roxy's camo jacket from the boot and started down the road towards the Sym-Bio-Tech site. The road turned right at the first bend, drifting away from her objective. She put the jacket on before stepping off the road.

It was only a couple hundred yards down the slope and across the field as she approached the side perimeter fence. If any of the science geeks in there were wistfully looking out of the window, none of them seemed to have noticed her or raised the alarm.

One of the structures along the perimeter was an electricity cabinet, clearly marked by danger signs on all sides. It was a large shed that gave Stephanie a few metres of space to operate without being spotted by the cameras. It also allowed her to sit just outside the motion sensor's range.

She took a moment to survey her surroundings. A short distance to her left, a row of industrial waste bins looked like a promising next step. Stephanie made a dash for them and flattened herself behind the largest one.

Another sprint took her to the corner of the facility. From

there, she could see the rear gate, where she counted two guards, possibly armed.

A short hedge coasted the side of the courtyard. Stephanie took advantage of it for cover while sneaking as close to the rear gate as she dared before resorting to appropriate distraction measures. This one, unorthodox as it was, was easily Stephanie's favourite. It was almost sad to know it wouldn't survive the day.

As she took it out of the backpack, the remote-control car was ready to go. Twelve firecrackers were strapped to it, and a bundle of inflammable fabric completed the set.

Time to shine, she thought. *Or explode, I guess.*

She aimed the car at the facility's wall, taped the controller to keep it steady, then lit the fuse. As she released it, she could only hope she had calculated the fuse length correctly, allowing the car to travel far enough before the explosion.

The sound of the crash against the wall came before the popping of the firecrackers, confirming her calculation. The noise echoed across the space, satisfyingly similar to the sound of firearms. Anyone used to the sound of shots fired wouldn't have been fooled by it, but whoever was at the gate was bound to check out the commotion.

Right on cue, the security guards at the gate glanced at the cameras before one of them left the post to check what was happening.

The silencer already equipped on her tranquilising gun, Stephanie moved quickly towards the gate, shot the lone guard standing at the entrance, then shut off the cameras with the interference pen.

The second guard was still intent on studying the remains of the toy car by the wall, glancing around in all directions except the one he came from. Stephanie silently walked up to him and fired a second time.

When the tranquiliser caught him on the back of the shoulder, she quickly closed the gap between them to hold him up. The tranquiliser was already starting to take effect. There was very little resistance the man could offer as she walked him back to his post.

She stacked the two unconscious men inside the booth, then glanced at the monitors. Most were focused on the exterior of the building, but cameras inside the facility were available to search and select.

With no time to do an inventory of all the rooms, Stephanie located the laboratories on the first floor. That's where she needed to go.

She quickly grabbed one of the guards' passes, his security jacket, and the cap that was part of his uniform, calculating that this should be enough of a disguise if she came across anyone on her way to the Skaara.

Leaving the backpack behind, as no security guard would have been believable wearing one, Stephanie stepped out into the open, pulled the cap's visor low on her forehead, then crossed the concrete yard and headed confidently towards the rear entrance of the building.

Waving the pass over the sensor, she heard the click of the door, which she pulled open on a long, brightly lit corridor.

When working with SafeOp, she could have always counted on a detailed briefing on the target location, exit routes, elevators, and a list of other irrelevant details that may or may not have saved her life. None of that information about Sym-Bio-Tech was available to her as she stepped through the door. To compensate for that, all her senses were dialled up to a hundred.

Before moving along the hall, Stephanie searched for the interference pen in her pocket and turned off the cameras. Whoever was on surveillance duty for the rear entrance would see a security guard staring out toward the parking lot. The image would linger on their screen for a long time.

Stephanie quickly headed to the door on the other end of the corridor. As she stepped through it, she barely had time to spot the elevator to her left, when a short, moustachioed man turned the corner and almost bumped into her.

Her finger already on the interference pen, Stephanie turned off the cameras, then aimed the gun at the unfortunate man, just as he was about to speak. As he fell onto the floor instead, Stephanie called the elevator.

It wasn't long before the door opened for her. Once inside, it was time for a change of appearance. She shed the guard's jacket, keeping the cap low on her face.

There was only a moment to pause during the slow journey to the first floor.

So far, so good, she dared to think.

Adrenaline coursed through her body, her muscles alive with the excitement. She had never felt more at home than on a field operation.

Stephanie took a deep breath. Even the confined spaces of the elevator couldn't trigger her claustrophobia when she was running on that kind of high.

When the elevator's door opened again, Stephanie was ready with the interference pen in one hand and the tranquiliser gun in the other. She almost expected Bennett to materialise, wise to her plan. Instead, the hall was empty.

She turned off the cameras, re-holstered her gun, and surveyed the surroundings.

Of the people walking down the hallway, nobody seemed too concerned with her presence. That was too good to be true – and far from a good sign. Once again, she had the impression her arrival was expected and somewhat welcomed.

Maybe I can turn this to my advantage, she mused.

A new plan taking shape in her mind, she went to intercept two white coats that happened to be heading in her direction. Her shoulder bumped into one of them just as she walked past, enough of a commotion to hide her hand as she slipped the man's pass out of his pocket.

"Watch where you're going, would you?" she uttered.

"I'm sorry," the man mumbled.

Stephanie pressed her gamble. "I'm here on business for Mr Cavell, and I don't appreciate people stumbling all over me. Make yourself useful instead. Where is the specimen?"

The mention of Cavell's name was sure to elicit some response, and the white-coated man did not disappoint. "Of course. It's the door at the end of the corridor," he said hurriedly, pointing to the hall on her left. "You were given a pass, right?"

"Just be sure to mind your own business," grumbled Stephanie, already walking away, the stolen pass tucked in her hand.

When she reached the door, she held the pass against the magnetic lock, faking confidence while holding her breath. Then, a subtle click. She exhaled in relief.

It was only when Stephanie opened the door that she realised how unprepared she was for the encounter.

She had steeled herself against the shadow of a past foe, braced for the looming presence of the alien menace, but the Skaara held in that laboratory was nothing like that.

Occupying a corner of a plexiglass cage, Gwyn was a ragged bundle of skin. Stephanie couldn't know if her condition was due to the long time spent isolated or to the experiments Sym-Bio-Tech had already carried out on her – likely both, she decided.

She closed the door behind her and used the broom she spotted in the corner to block the entrance. That taken care of, she moved closer to the cage to take a better look at the Skaara. Something flipped in her stomach as she did that.

Only a few months earlier, that same huddled shape had been perched behind her shoulders, making her the unwilling actor in the Skaara's plan for Earth's colonisation.

Part of Stephanie was screaming to run away as fast as she could and let the Cavells do whatever they pleased with that wretched thing. Maybe Lucy was right, and she should never have planned to free the Skaara on her own.

She closed her eyes and took a deep breath in. There was tension, and a hint of dread creeping into her chest. She exhaled, burying it beneath her resolve.

There's a job to do, she told herself.

A simple lock kept the small cage door closed. There must have been a key somewhere in the room, but Stephanie had no time to search for it. She found a paperclip on one of the desks, then put on a pair of latex gloves and set to work. Seconds later, the lock opened for her.

She didn't feel anywhere near ready for what came next. Flashbacks of the Skaara jumping at her were running through her head, memories of their previous encounter. It was as if Gwyn was already tugging at her mind, even while locked away in a cage. Keeping those thoughts at bay was getting harder as time ticked by.

She started as the door of the laboratory jerked behind her. Someone was trying to get inside.

Time's up.

She threw the lock aside and opened the small door, finally coming face to face with the old foe. "No funny moves, do you hear?" she said, hoping the crippled Skaara would at least understand her intention, if not her words. "I'm here to get you out, so I need you to trust me. And don't jump at me. Please."

There was another jerk at the door, followed by a voice calling out something Stephanie couldn't understand.

Meanwhile, Gwyn hadn't moved from her crumpled position. For all Stephanie knew, she could have been dead already. With no time to find out if that was the case, Stephanie reached inside and gently touched the frail, hairless body. She felt stirring, but nothing more. Reaching inside with both arms, she lifted the Skaara and pulled her out.

"I know you've been through a lot, but I need you to make an effort now," she said. "I need you to crawl under my jacket and stay there until we're out."

The voices outside the door had quietened. Stephanie expected reinforcements to arrive any second.

The Skaara wasn't moving.

Stephanie considered the options and immediately discarded the idea to make skin to skin contact with Gwyn to allow communication. Instead, she lifted her jacket and shoved the Skaara underneath.

It was with dread and relief that she felt Gwyn's limbs reach for her torso and slowly make their way around her waist, holding it steady, yet not tight. Stephanie had to remind herself to breathe.

The two layers of fabric that separated the Skaara from the

human were the thinnest of boundaries between the two worlds.

Closing the zipper of her jacket, Stephanie made sure the alien refugee was well concealed. Then took off her gloves and exhaled. For a moment, she remained still, trying to get used to that strange body pressed against hers.

One more deep breath helped her find her centre and get out of her own head. There was still a job to do, after all.

Slowly and silently, she took the broom off the door handle.

The cameras were still off in the hallway. She opened the door just enough to look outside and ensure the hall was empty. A second later, she stepped out, only to see two people dressed in grey overalls appear around the corner.

It took them a few steps to recognise her as an intruder. When they did, Stephanie had already drawn the gun. A tranquilising bullet hit each of them square across the chest in quick succession, the shock knocking them back as they slowly folded to the floor.

With no time to stand and wait for the elevator, Stephanie pushed past it towards the service stairs and made her way to the ground floor. As she reached the door at the bottom, she gently turned the handle and pushed the door to check the situation at the reception: four security guards and one receptionist were prepped and ready to bar her way.

She silently closed the door again.

She needed a new plan.

Let me go.

It struck Stephanie that it wasn't her own thought that had come to her mind. Gwyn had searched for and found a way to get in contact with her skin.

"Get out of my head," she whispered through her teeth, instantly regretting the needless risk of speaking aloud.

I can help. Let me go.

She knew she was still in control of her body, yet Stephanie felt her mind slipping away. With her hands in her hair, she fought the impulse to scream, desperate to get rid of the parasite clinging to her thoughts.

She forced herself to lean against the wall instead, grounding herself enough to think of the next right thing to do. Taking one deep breath after another, she brought her hands to the zipper of her jacket and opened it. It was all she could do not to take it off and throw it away, as she felt like her own skin was on fire.

Finally, Gwyn's body half crawled, half stumbled to the floor while Stephanie took a step away along the wall. Then the Skaara moved its slender, slithery body to the closed door and waited.

It took Stephanie a few deep breaths to regain her focus and understand what Gwyn was trying to tell her. When she did, she gripped the tranquilising gun and held it at the ready, although her hands were trembling enough to make it almost useless.

She opened the door to the lobby once again. Gwyn moved at a surprising speed for a victim of abusive experimentation, slithering out of the door and out of sight.

Stephanie knew she should have followed, yet she found it hard to move. When she eventually managed to steady her grip on the gun and step out into the open, it was apparent that Gwyn had everything under control already in a most distressing way.

In the middle of the reception area, Stephanie could clearly see the two security guards by the desk, while another pair was standing further near the door. The Skaara was already wrapped around the ankle of the closest pair. Stephanie wondered how he hadn't noticed something pulling at his leg when he turned around towards his colleague.

His colleague had noticed the movement and turned to see a terrified expression on his face. "Eric, what the hell?"

That was all he had time to say, though, as Eric quickly lifted the Taser gun against him. The shot went off with an accompanying shriek from the receptionist, who had just turned in time to see the shocked body of the guard fall to the ground.

The rest of the security guards had already drawn their Taser guns, tentatively aiming them at a brainwashed Eric, when Stephanie finally joined the party. She fired three shots, two of which caught them square in the chest.

As she watched them folding to the floor unconscious, Stephanie felt Gwyn rejoining her, wrapping herself around her leg, securely over her trousers. Even so, it was enough to make her falter. She took a deep breath, reminding herself that was a good thing. It was safer for the Skaara to be with her rather than unleashed onto the world. After all, the whole reason she had gone there was to break Gwyn out and get her to cooperate. If the Skaara stuck with her voluntarily, it could only be for the best.

Maybe Lucy wasn't completely wrong about this, she thought.

One more deep breath before focusing once again on the task at hand. There was one more thing to do before Stephanie could make her way out.

She made her way towards a terrified receptionist. "Would you know if Bennett is visiting today?" she asked.

A terrified pair of long eyelashes stared at her for a couple of seconds before nodding once, followed by a long, green-painted fingernail raised to point at someone behind Stephanie's back.

"I see," she replied, then added, "by the way, I'm awfully

sorry for this."

Stephanie then raised the tranquiliser gun and shot her point blank. The force of the impact sent the chair wheeling backwards as the receptionist fell unconscious.

"Are you quite done with the personnel?"

It was a voice she would have recognised amongst a million others and that she waited far too long to hear again. "Damien," she said. "How nice of you to drop in to say hi."

"I should have guessed you were going to pull a stunt like this," he replied, sporting an amused smirk as he waved casually at the surroundings. "You were always the meddlesome kind."

Stephanie gave him a tight smile. "It's one of my best qualities."

"Debatable," he commented, then turned serious. "Give it back," he ordered as his hand moved slowly to his gun, still clipped to his waist.

After dealing with a Skaara wrapped around her leg, talking with Bennett felt like a walk in the park. He was dangerous and manipulative, but he was human, and his tentacles didn't hack into your brain – not literally, anyhow. She could handle a manipulative human. She gave him a smirk. "You'll have to be more specific than that."

"You are in no position to crack jokes, Davis. Do as I say, and I may let you live."

She re-holstered her tranquilising gun and raised her hands. "You know, Damien, you used to be more fun."

He frowned. "And you used to be more dead. I liked you better that way."

She could see his grip getting steadier on his gun. She took a step forward and continued. "I tried that. Not my favourite."

Damien looked as tense as a coiled spring. "I don't think you get a say in that."

Stephanie took another step forward. "What's going on, Damien? Back in the day, you'd have just shot me instead of bargaining. Should I be flattered?"

With a further step, Stephanie was close enough to be able to spring and tackle him before he could raise the gun towards her, if she needed to.

Damien looked to be fully aware of her strategy. "Return the specimen, or this time I'll make sure you stay dead."

Her eyebrows raised in fake surprise, Stephanie let out a chuckle. "Wow, have you graduated in villain clichés since the last time we met?" she taunted him, then slowly moved her hand to the back of her belt.

Damien disagreed with that move. He raised his gun in a flash move. "Hands where I can see them, Davis."

Stephanie complied. "There is something Avis Carmen wants. If I give it to you, will you let the Skaara come away with me?"

"The beacon?"

Stephanie nodded. With a tight wave of the gun, Damien encouraged her to produce the black box, so she lowered one arm to reach behind her back. She brought forward the shiny black box, offering it to Damien. "Do we have a deal?"

The amused smirk reappeared on Damien's face. "I must admit, I underestimated you."

He grabbed the beacon from Stephanie's hands. Just as he did that, a shot exploded in the room, and Stephanie hit the ground. When she glanced at the entrance door, where the shot had come from, Roxy's figure was standing tall and steady, holding a rifle gun still aimed at Damien's writhing body.

"What the hell, Roxy!"

"Oh, come off it! It was only a tranquiliser. You'll get your chance to shoot him later," she fired back, glancing through the door as if expecting reinforcements to arrive at any moment. "We have to go, now."

Stephanie didn't wait to be told twice.

They rushed through the door and made for the fields, the Skaara still clinging to Stephanie's leg.

The clouds were gathering, and a light drizzle had started to fall. As they reached the bend in the road right by the woodland's edge, they sprinted for the car and hid behind it. The only sounds around them were the droplets of rain falling over the silent hill.

Stephanie shivered in her clothes. The camo jacket offered her an extra layer. However, rain had already started to seep through, and the cold was getting to her.

"Do you think they'll pursue?" asked Roxy, sneaking a peek over the hood of the car.

"Not sure," replied Stephanie. Something told her the Skaara was expendable in Avis Carmen's eyes – especially once they had acquired the black box. "Can you see anything?"

"Coast is clear," confirmed Roxy. "It doesn't make sense."

A rustle of leaves, and the coast became very crowded all at once.

"Are you sure they came this way?" said one voice. It was a young one, and he sounded annoyed.

"Pete, shut up," said a second voice, a deeper tone, resolute. Stephanie thought that was the man in charge of the pursuit.

The man's steps approached the car. She held her breath and knew Roxy was doing the same.

"Hamish?" a third voice. "We got incoming."

An exhale, then the leader again, "Shut up, I said."

"It's the boss, Hamish."

The steps walked away from the car. A few minutes of silence. Stephanie could hear a low mumbling but couldn't make out what the leader was saying in the comms. She considered asking Gwyn to intervene and take out the whole team, however she ditched the thought as quickly as it had occurred to her. She couldn't think that way. Gwyn was not a weapon, and she certainly wasn't going to make a habit of unleashing a mind-leach on operatives like that.

She turned to Roxy, and their eyes met. Stephanie slowly and silently gripped her gun, and Roxy steadied her hold on the rifle. With her left hand, Stephanie started counting down from three. She had got as far as one when the leader spoke again, "We're going back."

Frowning, Stephanie turned to see Roxy mirroring her puzzled look.

The youngsters following the leader were none the wiser about what was happening. "What, just like that?" one of them said.

The leader must have already started on his way back to Sym-Bio-Tech, since his reply came muffled through the distance.

"At least we're getting out of this miserable weather," said the second of the young operatives.

Footsteps and voices moved further until all Stephanie could hear was the rustle of vegetation around her. A cold shiver ran through her body, and she felt Roxy's hand on her arm. "Let's get in the car, yeah?"

As they settled inside, Roxy turned on the engine and put the heater on full blast. It was then that Stephanie felt something brushing against her ankle. Looking down, she saw Skaara's body had half dropped to the floor.

The rain was getting heavier, with its loud hammering on the windshield

Stephanie took Gwyn off her ankle and cradled her in her lap. Only after she completed the action did she realise she was touching the Skaara with her bare hands. She looked like such a thin and harmless thing. Stephanie couldn't bring herself to be scared of her anymore.

"Is that little thing what all this fuss was about?" asked Roxy, as she glanced at the Skaara while wriggling out of her wet windbreaker.

"This is the one," replied Stephanie, distracted by the way Gwyn's limbs fell to the side of the seat. Something didn't look right.

Roxy threw the windbreaker onto the back seat. "I hope her personality is better than her looks."

"It isn't," said Stephanie. She regretted it as soon as she said it, yet her mind was still busy figuring out what was wrong.

Gwyn was peacefully resting in her lap, enjoying unimpeded contact with Stephanie's skin, yet there was no intruding thought coming to Stephanie's mind. There was something else too: the Skaara wasn't moving.

She tentatively rested a hand on Gwyn's body. "Are you still there?" she asked.

There was no response. The Skaara just lay still.

Roxy's voice came to Stephanie as a background noise. "Is she okay?" she was asking. Stephanie ignored her. The Skaara wasn't moving or reacting in any way. After all Stephanie had been through, that felt like the ultimate joke. "No," she whispered, still poking the alien skin. "This is not how it ends, you hear me? Wake up!"

Nothing.

Stephanie cursed under her breath. If Gwyn didn't make it, the chances of stopping the Skaara from declaring war on Earth dwindled down to almost nothing. She couldn't let that happen.

Beside her, Roxy had already taken out the laptop. She reached for the fluffy flash drive in the glove compartment and started browsing through the material.

"Look for the experiment on benzodiazepines," said Stephanie. She had looked at the material only briefly, yet she remembered reading something about the effect of substances on the Skaara's physiology. It was the same experiment that had led to the discovery of tranquilisers as an antidote for their mind control.

Come on, you annoying little bugger, she kept on thinking, as if one of those thoughts could pierce the barrier and bring the Skaara back.

Seconds later, Roxy had found the report and was looking at the answer they needed. "Sodium bicarbonate," she burst out.

While Stephanie held on to the Skaara, wishing with all her might it wasn't too late already, Roxy reversed the car into the road, then sped off to retrieve a life-saving dose of baking soda.

- XI -

It was as if Matthew's parents couldn't lower themselves to stay in any place with less than six bedrooms and five bathrooms. Even if the Ducksworth summer house was clearly smaller than Partridge Manor, Lucy felt she'd need a map to find her way to the nearest exit.

After their arrival in the morning, the Cavells had been perfectly lovely, offering them tea and biscuits in the downstairs living room, making small talk about the weather and Matthew's latest career accomplishments. Lucy knew the conversation would shift soon – or at least hoped so.

Half an hour in, she decided to excuse herself and go look for a bathroom. It was just lucky one of Cavells' men caught her right outside the living room and offered to guide her. When she eventually made it back into the room, the conversation had moved onto Frank. The way everyone glanced at her when she sat back on the sofa, anyone would have thought she'd interrupted Frank's very own meeting with the in-laws.

While her brother explained his past life and history as if he had been a guest on the Late Night Show, Lucy's gaze reached the large window just behind Lady Partridge and her husband, where the low-hanging clouds threatened to overshadow the blue morning sky. Her attention, however, was regularly brought back to the room as she kept on sliding awkwardly on a leather sofa that had clearly been bought to torture unwanted guests. She wondered how Matthew, sitting right next to her, could look so unbothered by it.

Third in line on the same sofa, Frank had taken a perched position on the very edge of the seat. "The experiment is only a part of it," he was explaining. "What we're aiming to achieve is something with far-reaching applications in chemical engineering."

Lady Partridge sharply lowered her head into a quick nod. She was the human equivalent of a guitar string. Mr Cavell, sitting on the armchair to her right, seemed to capture all that tension and release it by fidgeting with anything he could get his hands on. For the moment, he was casually handling a teaspoon while basking in the icy glow his wife was giving. "Interesting," he said. "Have you thought of how you'll carry your work forward once your doctorate is completed? It'd be a shame to see all that potential wasted."

As Frank started to answer, however, Lady Partridge interjected, "My husband and I have invested in a number of ventures. We could use a keen intellect like yours."

"I'd be honoured to be working for you," Frank said politely. Lucy could hardly hide a grimace.

The corners of Lady Partridge's lips spread wider, leaving the rest of her face unaffected. Lucy decided that must have been her version of a smile.

Just as Mr Cavell was about to add something to the conversation, a bald man in a black suit walked in and grabbed everybody's attention. "What is it, Gerald?" asked Mr Cavell.

"A message from Herefordshire," he replied, then hesitated and only continued when Lady Partridge waved at him to do so.

"There's been a breach."

Lucy could sense the woman's eyes on her. She knew what Gerald's message meant, yet she wouldn't dare move a muscle.

"Have the assets been compromised?" asked Lady Partridge, ignoring the sharp tingling of the teaspoon Mr Cavell had dropped on the coffee table in front of him.

Gerald nodded, visibly uncomfortable at the crowd listening to his message. "I believe that's the case. Should we deploy security, ma'am?"

Lady Partridge turned a perplexed glare towards him. "Has Millican been contacted? He can deal with the security breach."

"He has," he said, then paused. Unlike before, he wasn't going to speak to the room. "Ma'am..."

"What is it, Gerald?" asked Mr Cavell, visibly annoyed at the man's hesitation.

"There's something else, sir."

Mr Cavell gestured for him to walk closer, and so he did.

Lucy tried her best to capture any word of the message, unsuccessfully. What she had heard, however, was enough to understand what had happened. There had been a breach in Herefordshire, where Davis was headed. She had done it. She had broken into the Sym-Bio-Tech facility and had taken Gwyn out. She only hoped the two hadn't started battling each other on the way home. The name Millican didn't ring any bells, though. She made a mental note to ask Davis about it as soon as they met again.

If we meet again, she thought, then pushed the thought away.

Once the second part of the message had been quietly delivered, Gerald vanished out of the room as swiftly as he had appeared.

While Mr Cavell's fidgeting had little abated after the news,

Lady Partridge was making a show of keeping her composure and gestured to resume the interrupted conversation. Lucy wasn't fooled by it, though. Her shoulders had lifted a little, her back was a touch straighter, and a small twitch played at the corner of her lips. She was satisfied, even happy about something.

What if Davis has been caught? thought Lucy. She couldn't even contemplate that scenario.

There wasn't much time to fantasise anyway, as Mr Cavell was ready to dismiss her. "Matthew," he said, spelling out each letter of the name, "Why don't you take your *lady friend* here for a walk around the back garden while your mother and I continue our chat with Frank?" He waved his hands towards the door, as if trying to get rid of some bad mojo. The tone he had used was a surprising kind of patronising from a man who moved as if he had ants in his suit.

She glared at him, defying the consequences of such an act, while Matthew darted to attention as if he had been given an order. "Sure," he said, then stood up and reached a hand to Lucy, who shifted her glare to the extended hand.

"I don't know, *Matthew*" – she spoke each letter of the name in her best impersonation of Mr Cavell – "I'm not sure your *lady friend* feels like having a walk in the rain."

Lady Partridge rolled her eyes while Mr Cavell disappointingly misunderstood the taunt. "It's only a drizzle, dear. Or should I think city girls like you lock themselves inside at any sign of bad weather?"

Lucy felt that, if they had been in the eighteenth century, he would've suggested she be treated for consumption.

Torn between his father and his girlfriend, Matthew stood awkwardly for a moment longer. Eventually, it was Lucy who made the decision for him, as she stood up and took his still proffered hand. "Let's go for a walk, Matthew."

He followed her without a word. Lucy thought he should have rejoiced at the lack of sharp objects within her reach, or she'd have probably stabbed someone she shouldn't have.

They walked silently down the hall until she felt Matthew grabbing her arm. She turned with a glare, only to see him point at the corridor to their left. "Fine, you lead," she grunted.

When they reached the conservatory, the pale light of the winter sun barely made it through the pane windows, while a drizzling mist still washed the colours of the landscape. The world outside looked like a painting, never betraying the icy temperatures that still engulfed the land in the early days of March.

Matthew loosely gestured at the wicker chairs stood by the side. "We can sit over here for a while."

"While you keep me occupied, so I don't ruin your parents' chat with Frankie, is that right?"

Matthew scoffed. "Why are you so annoyed about that?"

She wasn't annoyed; she was terrified about it. Her brother was sitting in the other room, being recruited and possibly brainwashed into something called Avis Carmen, whose purpose was basically to slaughter an extra-terrestrial species and build an empire on the spoils.

She couldn't tell him any of that, of course. "It'd be nice to walk in the garden, actually," she said instead.

"It's raining," replied Matthew matter-of-factly.

"I'll have to get my coat," she replied. "Would you mind waiting for me just a second?"

As she said the words, Lucy was already walking away, retracing her steps towards the living room, looking for the butler–slash–security details – because everyone working for the Cavell looked like they were part security guard – who could hand her jacket. It was on the way back to the conservatory that she caught Frankie's voice as he said, "A week is not long, but I'll do my best."

A week to what? she wondered. That didn't sound like a PhD project kind of deadline.

Lucy moved a couple of steps closer to the living room, pressing her back against the wall to stay out of sight, waiting to hear more.

"Mr Campbell, I'm sure you understand this is not like one of your lab experiments," came Lady Partridge's voice. "You'll have the resources, and you'll have the reports from the latest tests. We're expecting to see results in a week's time. It's bad enough that the pod is still stuck to the ground."

She was referring to the Skaara pod, no doubt. One of them must have survived the explosion intact. No wonder they hadn't been able to move it – those things were meant to stick to a spaceship hull through interplanetary space travel. It was possible to remove them, but someone would have to be taught. And Lucy had been taught. She knew how to take the pod from the ground and move it away. It would mean helping Avis Carmen, sure, but it would also allow her to be in the team – maybe even do some damage from the inside. She could be in the right position to do the right thing, for once.

Seeing Davis alive hadn't erased the guilt she felt for the harm she had caused. The pull of the redemption she could accomplish was too strong to resist, even if she had wanted to resist it.

Lucy was through the door before she could even register her own movement. Words flew out of her mouth, still as she asked herself why she was talking at all. "You better take me along, if it's the pod you're trying to crack. I'm probably the only one who knows how to move that thing around anyway."

Frank started at her entrance. "Luce, what are you doing?"

Lucy dismissed him with a wave. "Shut up, Frankie. The grown-ups are talking."

Lady Partridge's look felt like splinters of ice raining over her. "We appreciate your offer, Miss Campbell. However, we already have a team of experts on the case."

She wasn't even sure what good that was going to do, but she had to find a way to stick around instead of being whisked away to become the Demon Guy's pet project.

"The creeper herself taught me how to pick up the pod," she said, the temperature in her voice lowering to match hers. She paused, expecting an acknowledgement that never came. "Also, I happen to know where the missing beacon is hidden. I believe that could be of value."

"You what?" snapped Frank. Everyone ignored his outburst.

"I doubt that is true, girl. The beacon is exactly where it should be, and you clearly don't know where that is," interjected Mr Cavell.

Lady Partridge, however, hadn't moved. Lucy kept her gaze on her, like a staring competition she couldn't lose.

Finally, the Lady exhaled and shook her head. "Matthew has been asking to bring you along, and I suppose it would be useful to carry the pod away from the explosion site," she conceded. "If you insist, we'll allow you to follow the team, provided you share with us all information you have acquired on the pods and the Skaara. Do we have an agreement?"

Lucy nodded. "We do."

"Very well then," said Lady Partridge with an impatient wave.

"You better go tell the news to Matthew. The grown-ups still have a lot to discuss."

Lucy ignored the jab at her earlier comment. "Of course," she mumbled, almost unwilling to let her have the last word.

Once in the hall, she allowed herself to breathe. She glanced briefly at her brother. His jaw was clenched, and he had started rubbing the palms of his hands. She wasn't sure if he was angrier at her for hiding what she knew or for crashing his research party.

She made her way down the hall.

It's going to be fine, she told herself. As long as she kept on repeating that, she could at least pretend to believe it. Hero work wasn't for her. Davis was the hero, while Lucy just held on to whatever would keep her alive. Except her world had been turned upside down lately.

Matthew's voice from the end of the hall shook her out of her musings. "Did you get your jacket?"

"Yes, but I have to pee. I'll be right there."

She turned tail and headed back into the house. She only had to find a quiet enough place for herself, and the downstairs toilet was perfect for that. It only took her one wrong turn to find it again.

It wasn't until she lit up her phone's screen that she started doubting what she was doing. After all, she was in the room when the report came in, and all signs pointed to Davis having been taken.

She shook her head in an attempt to shake those thoughts away as well.

Paranoia isn't going to help anyone, she thought to herself.

Sending her a message was probably nothing more than pointless, yet she couldn't help it. She had to reach out.

She carefully wrote: *I hope you're okay. Party next weekend. I'm staying with Frankie until then.*

It was the cringiest message she had ever written, yet she wouldn't dare write anything that would give away who Amelie really was.

She pressed send, then stared at the screen for a few seconds. She knew there wouldn't be any response, certainly not so quickly, yet it still took her a minute to take her eyes off the screen and put the phone back in her pocket.

She was paralysed with fear, yet at the same time, it felt exhilarating. Her whole body felt like a spring ready to release, yet she wouldn't dare let go. She checked her hands and saw they were shaking. Leaning against the sink, she took a couple of deep breaths. When the buzz in her head had subsided enough for her to hear her own thoughts again, she flushed the toilet she hadn't used and made her way back to the conservatory to tell Matthew the big news.

The bathtub was filled with a solution of water and baking soda. The unconscious Skaara had been immersed in it for hours. After numerous checks, Stephanie still had to see any sign that Gwyn was still alive.

It had been a few hours already since Roxy had left – a bit too long for a simple grocery run, Stephanie thought. She had been left on her own to monitor the progress of the Skaara's recovery, and she was feeling more and more restless. It was like waiting for a bucket of water to boil while holding a lit match underneath it.

After renewing the solution a couple of times, she swapped baking soda for ammonia since the notes on the flash drive suggested it would be even more effective. Nothing, however, had brought any visible improvement.

Maybe she just had to give it time.

Maybe it was already too late.

If she had correctly decoded Lucy's message, Avis Carmen was planning to host the landing of the Skaara spaceship in only two days. They were running out of time.

The front door opened with a jingling of keys and closed with a thud. Stephanie moved to the landing and watched Roxy make her way down the hall. "You took your time," she said, throwing one last glance at the immobile shape of Gwyn in the bathtub before joining Roxy downstairs in the kitchen.

Roxy dropped three grocery bags on the table and started sorting the items to their place in the kitchen. "Yeah," she said slowly as she moved. "Sorry about that. Funny crowd at the shop today."

Stephanie looked up. "I don't see you laughing, though."

With a sigh, Roxy dropped a pack of pasta back in the grocery bag and looked straight at Stephanie for the first time since she had walked in. "I got the call-up," she said.

It took a moment for Stephanie to process what that meant. "Who was it?"

"Does it matter?"

Roxy had been away for the best part of two years, so she didn't see how that could be important. Stephanie, however, saw it differently. "Was it a woman, five-foot-three, brown hair, tired-looking? Did she talk like every other sentence is a Christmas celebration?"

"Spot on, why?"

Stephanie nodded to herself. "Victoria Evans."

"Great, do you also know her birthday? I'm dying to send her a card," commented Roxy, sarcasm dripping from her tone. Stephanie knew better than to answer. Instead, she waited a few moments for Roxy to calm down. "She asked me to bring you in," she added.

"We knew this was going to happen," replied Stephanie. "I'm surprised you weren't told to kill me."

Roxy sneered. "I was given the option. I picked envelope two instead."

As she had said, they had expected that to happen – still, Stephanie felt a hollow open in her stomach. For a moment, she watched Roxy resume her arranging of grocery items, then went to pick one of the bags to join in the effort.

Twice, Evans had kept her alive. Stephanie couldn't believe Avis Carmen cared too much about it, which meant Evans could be more of a friend than she had anticipated. "Did she mention Millican?" she asked, considering a box of chocolate biscuits.

"No," replied Roxy, stashing away the tea, "but Bennett's name came up a few times. Apparently, he's leading field operations."

"Lady Partridge is leading operations," countered Stephanie.

"Lady Partridge wouldn't dirty her fancy gloved fingers with something like that, and you know it."

Stephanie shook her head. Bennet couldn't be that important, she was sure. "Nothing happens without the Lady knowing about it. Bennet might be making plans, but he wouldn't be brushing his teeth if Lady Partridge said so.."

"I'm surprised he puts up with it, then," commented Roxy. "From what I hear, he's been all over the world, handling security operations. They try to make it look as if he's only organising site security."

"You think he's directing field operations abroad?" asked Stephanie, a bottle of Appletizer in her hand. "Why did you buy this, anyway?"

"Leave my Appletizer alone," warned Roxy, taking the bottle from her. "And yes. If he's not directing operations now, he must be preparing the groundwork for something big in the future."

Stephanie nodded. She had thought that much herself. "We can still take him down. You and I."

Roxy was placing the bottle in the fridge. She stopped midmotion. "Please tell me this has nothing to do with the girl."

"This has nothing to do with the girl," said Stephanie promptly, feeling the sting of the lie piercing her chest. It had everything to do with the girl. "Damien Bennett is a legitimised criminal. He killed my partner in São Paulo and almost killed me. If we get the chance to take him out, don't you think we should?"

Little surprise, Roxy saw right through her. She exhaled and closed the fridge. "They won't hurt her as long as they think she's one of their own. She's safe where she is, even with Bennett sniffing around."

"I know," said Stephanie, and it was true. Her brain knew Roxy was right, even if her heart was telling her otherwise. "Can you get yourself on the list for the landing party this weekend?"

"Do you have a plan?"

"Probably best if you don't know."

Roxy opened her mouth to whip her comeback, but her words never made it out, as something crashed somewhere above them, followed by a loud thud. They both knew what it meant.

Stephanie rushed up the stairs, all her senses alert.

A couple of plastic bottles had been thrown out of the door and were lying on the ground at the top of the staircase. Stephanie glanced at the two bedroom doors – both standing open.

"I'll check the bedrooms," offered Roxy, silently moving behind her.

Scanning the floor for signs of life, Stephanie approached the bathroom door and slowly moved to investigate the room.

The bathtub was empty, its plug pulled to drain the ammonia solution.

She took a step forward. There was no sign of Gwyn anywhere – or at least so she thought, until she felt something wrapping around her ankle. It was all Stephanie could do not to kick it away and scream. Instead, she remained still and looked down to see the Skaara lying on the floor, one limb stretched out to reach her foot. She wasn't even trying to gain access to her skin. She seemed content with merely being noticed.

A few days earlier, a Skaara loose in the room would have been one of the most threatening circumstances Stephanie could have envisioned. Things had changed significantly since that very morning, though.

Lowering herself to sit on her haunches, Stephanie gently took the Skaara's arm off her ankle. As their skin touched, a thought came rushing through.

It's a trap. You must stop them.

"Yeah, I figured that one out by myself," she murmured. "Is there anything else you have for me?"

Yes.

She exhaled. "Found her," she called to the hall behind her.

"Is she okay?" asked Roxy, emerging from one of the bedrooms.

Stephanie nodded. "We're going to need some coffee. It's going to be a long night."

It was a small team that Avis Carmen had dispatched to the landing site in the Forest of Dean, the place where the first Skaara spaceship had touched down no months than five months earlier - also the place where Lucy, Matthew, and Frank had first met the little space crawler that had changed their lives so dramatically.

The site had been under army control for a while, but only a skeleton crew had been left since the explosion that blew up the spaceship and half the camp. Avis Carmen's objective was to retrieve the only Skaara pod that had survived the devastation – a pod that had been stuck to the ground ever since Edward Cook had placed it there.

Lucy barely recognised the place when they reached the landing site. Everything around the hangar had been flattened, as if the big bad wolf had blown over the marquees and thrown everything to the ground. Memories of her last moments there came rushing in, and she could almost see Davis walking towards her amongst the rubble.

She closed her eyes and tried to breathe the thought away.

She let Matthew and the rest of the team make their way through the debris of the explosion and into the site to confirm all necessary permissions. She had no rush to see the wreckage hidden behind the hangar wall – the only wall that had been left upright. She didn't want to spend a second longer than necessary around that place at all.

Lucy checked her phone once again.

It wouldn't kill her to send a thumbs-up or something, she thought, well aware that a text reply might indeed mean Davis's life or death if intercepted.

When Matthew knocked on the car window, Lucy almost dropped her phone.

"We're almost ready," he said, his voice coming muffled from the outside.

Reluctantly, Lucy opened the door and got out of the car. The smell of burnt wood was still in the air, soft and tangy like that November day they had hiked through the wood to find the spaceship. She was tempted to hold her breath.

As she approached, the hangar's wall stood deceptively intact in front of her, concealing the destruction on the other side.

"Why haven't they taken all this away already?" she asked Matthew, who had been tasked to lead her to the pod.

"They haven't found a way to do that yet," he explained. "The metal of the spaceship has fused with everything else around it, including the ground. Weird thing is, the explosion was cold. Frankie understands this better than me, but I was told there was no fire and smoke, only a big boom and a lot of wind. Some kind of fuel the Skaara must have had in there to make that happen."

Lucy didn't reply. All she could think was that Davis had been caught in that big boom and survived – barely.

As they turned the corner, Matthew's explanation took a whole new meaning. What had been the inside of the hangar had turned into a continuous surface of solid metal which, at its edges, transitioned seamlessly into earth, like tempered glass that slowly grew more and more riddled with impurity. The flawless lucidity of the metal became dustier, shiny black into granular ochre, the closer it got to the ground, until it was impossible to tell the difference from the actual earth. Lucy had never seen anything like it.

"The pod is right over here," said Matthew, waving her to the side of the former hangar. When Lucy stepped beside him, he pointed at something amongst the rubble. "The team has been looking at it from all angles and ran out of options. Short of taking out the whole square of ground it's anchored on, nobody really knows what to do, and the National Trust still have to give us permission to do that, so we've been looking for a quicker alternative. Do you really think you can take it off the ground?"

Judging from his tone, he didn't believe she could.

Time to show him.

Without a word, she made her way to the small football-sized Skaara shell, the air thick with anticipation. She recognised the foamy substance at its base, recalling what Edward Cook had taught her. Then she pictured Avis Carmen's scientists trying to scrape it off with a shovel and almost laughed out loud. Ridiculous.

What they didn't know was that the foam hid a suction mechanism at the bottom, which worked in concert with a gravitational magnet placed inside the pod. All standard equipment for Skaara interplanetary delivery. A Skaara-controlled Edward Cook had told her that much.

She knelt beside it and dipped her hands into the foam, just like she had been shown all those months before. She kneaded the base of the pod until she felt a soft pop coming from it. Only then did she take her hands off the foam and gently lift the pod off the floor.

The relief was enough to spread a grin all over her face.

"Miscreant," she said with a smirk as she carried her trophy past Matthew.

"Shame on me for ever doubting you," he replied with a warm smile, and for a moment, Lucy felt sorry for everything she was hiding and scheming behind his back. After all, being involved with a murdering crowd didn't necessarily make him a bad person. Maybe.

Frank popped his head out of the nearest SUV, interrupting her musing. "You did it?"

His eyes were wide in disbelief, as if he couldn't comprehend how the Skaara pod could be in Lucy's hands.

"Maybe it needed a woman's touch?" she commented.

He left the car and took the pod from her hands. "Is that your way to hog all the glory while everyone else does the actual work?" he retorted.

Lucy was about to snap back at him but saw his cheerful smile as she turned around, so she smiled back. "You know me so well."

"Frank, cut it out," interrupted Matthew as he joined them. He had misunderstood the tone, and the smirk on Frank's face had disappeared too quickly for him to notice. His face grim, Frank mumbled an apology and turned to place the pod in the back of the car. Lucy wanted to intercede, but Matthew had quickly moved on to a group of agents standing around another of the SUVs.

She should have said something to her brother, yet the words were failing her – siding against Matthew in any way seemed like a good way of putting off the only person who genuinely wanted her there – so she opened the door of the SUV instead and climbed inside, shutting the noise out.

Leaning back against the headrest, she closed her eyes and breathed. When she opened her eyes again, she checked her phone: no new notifications.

She had no idea what was going to happen that weekend. As far as she knew, the countdown to the end of the world had just started, and she dreaded to think she had just helped it along.

* * *

Hours of driving later, the car stopped in a farmyard somewhere in the Midlands. Lucy had done her best impression of a sleeping log for the whole journey and kept up her pretence when Matthew nudged her awake to lead her inside.

Even during the night, she only managed a few hours of sleep. In the early hours of the morning, as she lay awake in bed next to Matthew, she listened to him breathe deeply and quietly. The darkness of the room seemed to invite her to action.

It was only four in the morning. Lucy quietly got up and left the room to brave the cold night outside.

Davis still hadn't given her any response. Lucy considered sending another text, maybe even giving her a call, even though she knew how stupid and dangerous that would be for them both. The pit in her stomach only grew larger the longer she wondered about the reason for Davis's silence. Hungry for answers, Lucy found Victoria's number, which was saved on her phone, and dialled.

"Who's this?" came Victoria's voice. She sounded wide awake.

"Lucy. Lucy Campbell."

"For the love of peanuts! What are you thinking, calling me

like this!"

"I couldn't sleep," explained Lucy, measuring her words. "I'm nervous about today, and about Davis. I just wish I'd know if she was up to something."

A pause. If anyone was hidden in the darkness around her, Lucy wondered what they would think of that call.

"Davis won't be a problem to *you*, Miss Campbell. I can assure you of that much."

She must have been captured – or killed. Lucy couldn't think of any other reason Victoria would sound so confident. She took a deep breath, then exhaled. "Thank you, Evans."

The line, however, had already gone dead. Lucy hung up and headed back inside, a heavy weight on her chest and around her shoulders, yet ready to pretend she had never left the room at all.

* * *

The smell of coffee drifted all the way to the bedroom and woke Lucy up. Startled, she sat up in bed. The exhaustion must have gotten to her eventually, sending her to sleep at first light.

A pale sun was shining through a thin blanket of clouds out of the window, and there was chatter coming from the ground floor, mixing with the odd bird chirping outside.

Matthew had already left the room.

After a quick shower and a change of clothes, Lucy walked down to the kitchen, expecting nothing but busybodies getting ready for the Skaara's arrival that evening.

What she did not expect was Damien Bennett sitting at the kitchen table.

"Good morning," he greeted her as she walked in. He had

clearly been waiting for her.

"Morning," she responded.

He nudged a mug of coffee towards her. "I heard you get up. I thought you'd want some."

Lucy glanced at the cup of coffee, certain it must be poisoned. "Where's everybody?" she asked.

"In the yard, preparing a welcome gift," he replied, then pushed the coffee mug an inch closer to her.

Lucy picked up the offer, more and more certain she shouldn't drink it.

"I wish I could stay and chat, but I better join them," she said quickly. "My brother might need some help with the pod." She faked a disappointed smile to go with it – alas, duty called.

Damien seemed unfazed. "Of course. You'll find him in the barn." Then, as Lucy turned and made to leave, he added, "It's admirable, isn't it? His commitment, I mean. He insisted he'd be the one from the research team to be on site today. There was no persuading him otherwise." He paused, shook his head lightly, then raised his gaze to Lucy. "You'd almost think he was up to something, don't you think?"

Shit, she thought. *He's baiting me, I know it.*

She held Damien's gaze as she searched for a way out. "I wouldn't know," she replied eventually. "I'm afraid you'll have to figure that one out on your own."

"No, it's not like Frankie to be devious," he said, shaking his head. "He's a principled person. I doubt he'd even know how to tell a lie."

"That's my brother, alright," commented Lucy. She shifted her weight from one foot to the other, worried about whatever Damien was leading up to. "Well, I better go find him," she added, eager to leave the room before the conversation could go any further, afraid Damien could translate her words into a confession of guilt on her part.

"Before you do that," he called as she turned into the hall. She took a step back to look into his ice-blue eyes. "James Partridge joined us this morning. He set up shop in the living room down the hall. I heard you grew quite fond of him during your short visit. Maybe you want to go say hi?"

"Maybe I will." She held his gaze a moment longer, watching his lips unfurl into a grin. It was a rather unnerving sight. Lucy turned away from it and made her way down the hall.

Uncle Jim's white mane of hair was as unruly as Lucy remembered it. He was slouching on his desk, a screen full of overlapping windows lit up before him.

"I told you it won't be ready until later," he said as she walked in, wooden boards creaking under her step.

"Then what about a little break in the meantime?" she said.

Uncle Jim swivelled around so quickly that the feet of the chair dragged on the floor. "What are you doing here?" he asked. His tone was worried, yet Lucy was sure there was some relief in his eyes.

She smiled at him. "I asked nicely?"

They were silent for a moment. Lucy assumed there were eyes and ears everywhere in the house. There wasn't much she could say without giving herself away, and she couldn't be too sure Uncle Jim could be an ally.

Then, as if he had read her thoughts and meant to dispel her doubts, he reached for something on his desk and handed it over to her. "Here," he said. "Have a look at this. Do you notice something?"

Lucy took the black beacon from Uncle Jim's hands. It was the same shape and size as the beacon she had given Davis, yet it wasn't the same. There was no pulsing, and the blackness had a pastel feel to it.

"It's different than I remembered," she said cautiously.

Uncle Jim nodded, his eyebrows raised as if encouraging her to step forward towards her conclusion.

It's a fake, she thought, although she wouldn't dare say it out loud.

He must have read the realisation on her face as he sat back on his chair. "Things might turn out okay after all," he said.

Lucy looked at him through knitted eyebrows. "No," she said. "This doesn't change anything. They'll still find a way."

"Maybe you're right," he replied, "but don't you think this gives us a bit of hope?"

Hope had always felt a treacherous and capricious thing to her. She handed the fake beacon back to Uncle Jim. "I think hope is not enough to make things right. See you later, Jim."

She left the room before the feeling in her chest could reach her throat.

It was Davis's doing, no doubt about it. She must have made a copy of the beacon and sold it to Damien as the real thing. It meant Avis Carmen couldn't control where the spaceship would land, yet it wouldn't prevent them from finding out eventually.

The beacon swap was a smart move, but it only delayed the inevitable. Lucy wondered if Davis had planned anything after that – if she was even still alive for that.

Of course she's still alive, she thought. She had to be. Lucy simply wasn't ready to grieve her again.

She had to find her brother. Damien's words had spooked her. She was sure he wasn't above accusing Frank of some misdeed or other only to get to her.

As she walked out in the open air of the farmyard and towards the barn, she wondered what would have been worse: getting herself caught by the secret spy on duty or throwing the suspicion on Frank and having him booted out of a criminal organisation – something that could possibly involve his death, if Avis Carmen was as concerned about human lives as they were about extra-terrestrial ones.

Hard choice.

If only Davis had responded to her message. If only she had been around to do her hero thing.

She was barely aware of her hands closing in tight fists as she approached the barn's door. The space had been converted into a makeshift laboratory, which fundamentally looked like three tables covered with most of the tools Frank had put on his Christmas list since he was eight years old.

They had never been a team, Frank and her, not in the conventional sense of the term at least, but they had always looked after each other. Things had shifted when Lucy and Matthew had started going out together – a hint of jealousy at the exclusivity that Frank couldn't have anymore. Then the Skaara landed in the Forest of Dean, and everything had changed for good.

She closed her eyes for a moment, and the next thing she knew, Frankie had been recruited into the Avis Carmen operation, with generous sponsorship from his best friend Matthew.

Lucy hesitated at the threshold. Frankie leaned over the alien pod, unaware of her presence. She unclenched her fists, relaxed her shoulders, and stepped forward into the barn. "Need any help?"

He jerked upright, then frowned at her in contempt. "Maybe knock next time?"

She moved closer to have a better look and noticed the pod

was open. It reminded her of a flower, with its half a dozen pointy petals jutting outwards into the air. She couldn't see what was inside.

"Is it a boy?" she joked.

Frank threw her a sideways glance, purposefully ignoring her comment. He had never been much for conversation while tinkering with his toys.

"How does it work?" she tried again.

He kept on working on the pod in silence.

"What, you're just going to ignore me, now?" she insisted.

"I'm not supposed to talk about it," he explained, his eyes trained on the solution he was mixing.

"You mean they asked you not to tell me."

Frank looked up, only briefly. "It's sensitive, Luce. The whole operation hinges on this."

It wasn't just Damien, then. Matthew's parents must have also decided she wasn't to be trusted. "Frankie, it's me. You know you can trust me."

Lucy thought he was going to go on ignoring her. Instead, he explained, "The Skaara were using pods to spread some kind of spore, probably to convert the environment to something more suitable for them."

"Something that would also affect humans?" she interjected.

"Possible," he conceded. "In any case, we can use the spring mechanism and remove the spores without affecting the pod. It's a fascinating piece of organic technology, really."

As much as Lucy generally loved Frank's enthusiasm, Damien's words still echoed in her mind. "You better be careful, or someone might think you like these little space jerks," she cautioned him.

Frank looked at her for the first time since she walked in. "I appreciate their technology. It doesn't mean I want them to take over the world."

He said that slowly, with no trace of hate or anger in his voice. A few months earlier, the same man had arrived at the landing site with a backpack full of explosives, ready to blow up the whole base to get rid of the space invaders, fuelled by anger and fear. Lucy considered the difference, unsure if it meant an improvement at all.

"You know," he continued, "Lady Partridge was quite impressed at how well I'm getting on. Skaara tech is actually easy once you figure out the basic principles."

He sounded proud of himself, like a child who just got a gold star from his teacher. It would have been endearing if a whole species hadn't been threatened by it.

"What's the plan, then?" she asked.

"Why do you want to know?" he asked in return.

Everyone knew the spaceship would land that evening, yet only a handful of people had been told Avis Carmen's plan once the Skaara touched down on Earth. The effectiveness of the beacon swap depended heavily on what that plan was.

She shrugged, then said dismissively, "Because if Matthew trusts me enough to take me here, maybe I should know what we're doing, don't you think?"

Frank, however, wasn't going to give in easily. His loyalty to Matthew had become absolute since he had joined Avis Carmen. "Don't know, Luce. If he hasn't told you, there must be a reason."

"He probably just thought I wouldn't be interested," she insisted. Her brother looked at her askance. Lucy pressed on. "He's been under a lot of stress lately. I bet his parents have all sorts of impossible expectations. If I knew what the plan was, maybe I could help. I mean, I worked with the little buggers. I've seen how they operate."

She had kept her gaze on the ground, tracing the edge of the table as she spoke. She wasn't sure it would work, but Matthew was her only leverage.

Eventually, Frank conceded with a sigh. "Fine. We're replacing the alien spores with benzodiazepines."

"Hold on. I thought benzos were poison to the Skaara," burst Lucy, conscious as she spoke of the potential misstep she was about to make. She rushed to recover by adding, "How's the Lady going to figure out their secrets if she kills them all?"

"As I said, Luce, I'm getting a pretty good hang of their tech, and there's a whole team of engineers ready to dissect the spaceship. The Lady will do just fine," he said, returning to his work as he dipped a gloved hand into the pod once again.

Lucy stood, momentarily stunned. She knew Avis Carmen wasn't planning for a peaceful resolution, but slaughter on landing was a different level of evil. The Skaara wouldn't stand a chance. They'd be the authors of their own extinction the moment they found the pod and triggered the poison dispersion.

"Frankie, have you considered that a lethal dosage may not be a good idea?" she asked probingly.

He stopped working and looked at her once again. "Luce, I know what you're thinking, but you have to trust me on this one. This is the right thing to do."

"No, it's not," she protested, conscious of the thin line she was walking between giving herself away and convincing her brother of the terrible mistake he was making. "Couldn't you just knock them out? Don't you think that'd be better than a bunch of dead aliens?"

There was one person in the world Lucy had never managed to lie to, and Frankie knew that very well. He seemed to study her face for a sign of her bluff. She raised her eyebrows, urging him to believe her and see reason. All she wanted was for him not to become a murderer.

"It's too late for that, and too risky," he decided eventually. "I could get the dosage wrong. We don't have solid data on what is sufficient to do that. If we don't neutralise the crew, they could take over the whole Avis Carmen operation in a matter of days, and we'd barely notice."

Lucy scoffed. *Like that would be a bad thing*, she thought, then regretted even considering the idea.

"Since you have all the answers, I'd better leave you to it," she said.

He waved a hand and hummed a response that Lucy didn't understand. She lingered a moment longer, then turned and left the barn, walking back into the murky day outside and wondering what to do next.

The pod has to go, she thought. She was sure Avis Carmen would find some other way to eliminate the Skaara, but getting rid of threat number one seemed like a step in the right direction, together with finding someone else who realised the brutality of that plan.

Matthew was the next name on her list for that purpose, if he could even consider challenging his parents on the matter of mass murder.

Unfortunately, it was Damien who pushed himself off the wall of the farmhouse and approached her silently, a sly grin on his face. He had been waiting for her.

"Is Frankie doing okay?" he asked.

"You wouldn't believe it," she replied, with every intention of pushing past him.

Damien, however, stepped right in her path. "Care to take a walk with me?"

Not if you paid me for it, she thought. "Sure," she said instead.

As they silently made their way towards the open field behind the barnyard, Lucy looked around in search of someone – anyone, *anything* – she could use to get away from him. Even a squirrel in a tree would do. The coast was uncannily clear.

She put her hands in her pockets to hide her uneasiness. After all, Damien could have just wanted to talk to her, ask more questions about Frank. Somehow, she didn't believe that was the case.

"You must be wondering where your friend Davis is cooped up," he started.

Lucy almost stumbled. It could have been a harmless jab, or it could have meant he knew what Lucy had been up to. Nothing about Damien suggested the harmless option. "I trust Avis Carmen has prepared a suitable welcome party," she replied, trying to sound convincingly acquiescent to the cause.

"I wonder what she would think of all this," he continued.

Damien must have been testing her. "She thinks this whole operation has no regard for the planet's safety," she replied.

"Yes, that sounds like her," he commented amiably. "Do you agree?"

The friendly tone of the conversation was unsettling. Lucy carefully chose her words. "I think Davis has been cursed with a hero complex as big as her ego," she said. "She decided Lady Partridge is the villain, and nothing is going to change her mind."

Damien chuckled at that. "Funny you should say that," he commented. "Especially considering how helpful she's been to us in the last few days. I thought I owed you thanks for that, or was I mistaken?"

"Maybe you should," she said, trying to figure out what kind of help he might have been talking about.

Lucy knew Damien was trying to trick her, yet she remembered how satisfied Lady Partridge had looked when news of Gwyn's escape reached her – as if Davis's intervention had brought good news to the table.

They walked in silence for a few moments. Damien looked calm and in control, his pace slow and leisurely. Even so, Lucy felt he was about to pounce on her like prey.

The sound of their footsteps was the only thing she could hear, while a breath of cold wind made her wrap herself tighter in her jacket. "Is there a reason you brought me here or is it just part of your morning routine?" asked Lucy in an attempt to dispel the tension.

"Everything I do has a reason, Miss Campbell," he replied. The way he used her last name, it sounded like a death sentence.

A bit further up, a brick-layered structure stood straight in their path, like an ominous promise of things to come. It looked like a trap, and it smelled like a trap. One Lucy had already fallen into, right up to her neck.

As they reached the entrance, Damien grabbed an old key from a hook on the wall, opened the door, and produced a gun from under his jacket.

Of course he has a gun, she thought, and she almost blamed herself for not seeing it coming.

"In you go, let's make this quick," he said, gesturing for her to get inside.

Lucy had no choice but to step through the door. He followed her inside, closing the door behind them.

The space inside was empty and small. Lucy didn't think it looked one inch bigger than Matthew's living room, except dustier and rustier. The only window was a small aperture near the ceiling, on the opposite side of the entrance. In terms of exit routes, there weren't any.

"Where's Davis?" asked Damien as soon as the door was closed behind them.

"I have no idea. Costco, maybe?" replied Lucy promptly.

Damien took a step forward. "Spare me your jokes. She's up to something, and you've been helping her. Tell me what she's up to, and maybe I won't kill you."

Lucy took a step backwards. "Hey, hold the villain talk, would you? I have no idea what she's up to. As far as I know, she might have changed her mind and signed up with your people. Maybe she's leading her own task force at this very moment. Maybe Matt's mother has finally figured out she's way better than you at this whole shtick."

Damien flinched at the last part.

She had wanted to think her tone sounded confident, yet a tremor in her voice threatened to give her away. She was, in fact, terrified. She could only hope that Damien would misunderstand her nervous trembling for ill-concealed outrage.

"You think you can rattle me, don't you?" he said with a smirk. "Two can play that game. Or haven't you noticed the toy Uncle Jim has been playing with? Davis gave me the beacon. She offered it to me. The last piece of the puzzle, and she gave it up like she didn't care. Maybe you overestimated her after all."

"Why are you so worried about her, then?"

He chuckled. "I'm not going to trust her until she's dead. And the same goes for you."

He raised the gun, and Lucy's mind went blank. If there was ever a moment for a hero to sweep in and save the day, that was it. She held her breath.

This is it, she thought. *I can't believe I survived an alien landing for this.*

"The beacon is a fake," she blurted out, survival instinct taking over her common sense.

"Lies won't get you anywhere," commented Damien. As he held the shot, Lucy breathed in hope.

"It would explain why Davis was so willing to share, don't you think?" she insisted, trying hard not to break eye contact.

Damien didn't falter. "Where's the real one?"

Lucy exhaled. "I don't know," she countered.

There was a pause. Lucy almost expected a shot to explode, the bullet ripping through her chest.

To her surprise, however, Damien was hesitating. "Is she coming here today?"

"Maybe," insisted Lucy. "I think she wants to kill you more than she wants to save the world. Maybe that's her plan. Maybe she's been tailing you this whole time. Does that sound like what you wanted to hear?"

As she said that, Victoria's words came back to her. *Davis won't be a problem to you*, she had said.

"Much obliged," he replied, that smirk returning to his face. "You'd have been more useful if you could have pointed us to the real beacon, but telling us about the fake is just as good. This way, you'll die knowing the invaluable help you've given to Avis Carmen."

Listening to Damien's words, all Lucy could feel was the numbness spreading from her chest. Even the threat to her life wasn't enough to shake her out of that.

Just then, however, the door opened behind Damien, and the most unlikely hero swooped in: Victoria Evans.

She was the last person Lucy had expected to see walking in to stop Damien's one-man firing squad. "I wouldn't do that if I were you," she said.

"Evans, get out of here. This is none of your concern," he rebuked her.

Lucy watched the scene unfold as if it weren't her life on the line. Her thoughts were still on Davis and the fake beacon she had just revealed.

Victoria, however, wasn't going to argue about her orders. "The instructions were to lock her away, not to put a bullet in her head. Do you think young Cavell would be grateful to you for that?"

"The young Cavell, maybe not, but I bet the lady of the house would give me a promotion for that," he fired back.

Victoria's gaze, however, was unwavering. "You will follow orders, Bennett, or you know you'll regret it. The girl can still be of use."

A moment, then Damien sighed, the same a child would when told to finish his homework before going to the playground. As if murder was his idea of fun. "Fine," he conceded, then turned to Lucy, a disappointed look on his face. "I don't agree with it, though."

"Of course you don't."

He turned to Lucy, a disappointed look on his face. "You stay put," he said. "I'll come pick you up once we're done."

Lucy stood motionless. When the door was bolted shut, she let her knees bend and found herself kneeling on the ground, where she remained for a long time.

- XIV -

There was no one in sight as Stephanie approached the farmhouse from the southern side. The bad news was that vegetation offered her cover only as long as she stayed on the road, while the ground separating her from the farm was a long hundred yards or so of bare land.

Even with the windy and cloudy weather on her side, it wouldn't be easy to make an approach unnoticed.

It was little intel that Roxy had managed to gather for her. Her assignment for Avis Carmen had nothing to do with the scheduled landing. Dropping her off in the vicinity of the farmhouse was the only help she could give. Stephanie had taken it, together with half of Roxy's kit.

Using a pair of binoculars, she counted three men walking the front yard of the main house. Three SUVs and Victoria's green Fiesta were parked beside a birch tree. She was expecting at least three more agents walking the property, and one of them would be Damien Bennett.

A thought drifted in: *I can help with the first round.*

"I won't have you walking around in someone else's brain," whispered Stephanie. "You stay put."

Wrapped around her waist, Gwyn had earned the privilege of a small patch of skin they could use to communicate. Un-

164

beknownst to the Skaara, Stephanie had also spread some benzodiazepines on a protein bar she kept in one of her pockets – for old time's sake, so to speak.

Surveying her surroundings, she identified a couple of spots that could give her temporary cover on her run towards her target. The first one was a thin bush just a quick sprint away. Stephanie took a deep breath and covered the distance.

She held her breath as she sat motionless, listening for any shout of alert.

Everything remained quiet in the countryside around her.

To her left, an apple tree had stubbornly survived the years after the orchard had been abandoned. It wasn't a lot of cover, but she could still get away with it, with some luck.

Another deep breath and another sprint. Stephanie reached the small tree and flattened herself behind it. Then she heard, "Hey, did you see that?"

She waited, hoping the man would decide he imagined it.

"There's something behind that tree," another voice said.

Stephanie didn't need to hear the steps approaching to know they were coming for her.

"Fine, you win. Go," she whispered.

She had barely finished the sentence when she felt Gwyn's body move under her jacket and slide away from her. A few seconds later, the man's voice spoke again, "Must have been a bird. There's nothing there."

"You've got to get your eyes checked to think there was anything there at all," the second voice replied.

Stephanie silently exhaled. Listening to the footsteps retreating, she waited until she felt the weight of the Skaara on her thigh.

They'll be distracted for a short time. You must be quick.

"Time to storm the castle, then."

She checked to see the two men walking away from her, then left her hiding spot and sprinted to the wall of the farmhouse, careful to turn the corner and stay out of sight. As she pressed her back against the wall, she surveyed the backyard: a small round stone structure stood a few yards away while a few trees were spread around the green grass. Nobody was stationed there for surveillance. Feeling for the knife tucked in her belt, she made sure it was easily accessible should anyone turn the corner and surprise her.

Stephanie made her way alongside the wall.

Leaving Damien with the fake beacon had bought them some time – a sorely needed reprieve, since Gwyn was certain they were using the only surviving Skaara pod to plan an ambush. Stephanie had no way of knowing what that would entail, and she wasn't eager to find out. She had to find that pod and destroy it before it could cause any damage.

Ducking under the first window she encountered, she peeked inside, only to see an empty room and a clear table. She moved on.

Another window and a surprise guest behind it: James Partridge sat hunched over some papers, scribbling away. Next to him, the black box Stephanie had given Damien. Partridge must have realised it was a fake and decided to play along regardless.

She considered tapping on the window to attract his attention, then reconsidered. It was safer to have Roxy reach out to him instead, should the need arise.

Finding the back door closed, she skipped across it to reach the next window in the line. As she glanced inside, she recognised Matthew standing by the door. He had his back to the room, and judging from the way he moved, it looked as if he was talking to someone just out of sight.

As she pressed on, she found the barn just around the corner. Between that and the small structure behind her, Stephanie had to guess where Avis Carmen had set up the workshop and where they were keeping the secret weapon.

Someone was shouting orders in the yard. A moment later, as if on cue, a familiar face appeared from the barn door. Frank Campbell stood there for a second, a puzzled frown on his face, then called out, "It'll be ready in a minute!"

He must have been the one working on the weapon. Stephanie couldn't think of any other reason for him to be there.

After checking the surroundings, she moved further around the corner, enough to see that she could have made it to the side door without being seen. She dashed for it, then flattened herself against the wall, listening for any reactions.

Nobody seemed to have seen her nor heard her movements.

She was about to open the door when a familiar voice caught her attention.

"I still think we should have killed her."

It was Damien Bennett walking away from the barn. He was talking to Victoria, who quickly rebuked him, "And I still think you're paid to follow orders."

"Just pray I never find out you've been double-crossing us, Evans. I'm not paid to like you."

Stephanie watched them walk out of sight. Whoever they were talking about was none of her concern. Not with the Skaara pod now within her reach.

As footsteps moved farther, Stephanie pushed the door to the barn open and snuck inside.

Frank stood by a large table littered with tools, pots, and beakers. In the middle of it was an egg-shaped object that

Stephanie immediately recognised as one of the Skaara pods. The last time she had seen one of those, there was an entire cargo hull packed with them, and she was about to blow them all up.

After Gwyn had told her Avis Carmen's plan, Stephanie had hoped they hadn't been able to crack the Skaara technology, revelling in the possibility the pod had remained impenetrable and unaltered, or at least stuck to the ground by the remains of Gwyn's spaceship.

In an attempt to have a better look, Stephanie brushed against a shovel and caught it just in time to stop the fall. The move, however, was still loud enough for Frank to hear.

The look of surprise on his face lasted a whole second before he found words to say, "What are you doing here?"

He was clearly not worried about being heard. Stephanie brought a finger to her lips to ask for his silence. "You have to come with me," she whispered.

Frank kept on staring. "What are you doing here?" he insisted, still rooted to the spot. His voice had at least got closer to a whisper.

"I'm here to take you somewhere safe," she said, holding up the shovel she had just saved from toppling over. She realised it wasn't giving the right impression, so she leaned it back against the post. "Have you managed to open that thing?" she asked, waving at the Skaara pod on the table behind Frank.

Frank scoffed. "Of course. I opened it, prepped it, and then closed it again. It's all ready to go."

Not the news Stephanie wanted to hear. "What do you mean you prepped it?" she asked.

"Repurposed," he clarified. "My sister is not the only one who knows how to deal with these things."

That still didn't explain. The mention of Lucy, however, brought something else to Stephanie's mind. She glanced at the door, wondering how long she had left before someone walked in. "Lucy wasn't working with you then. Do you know where she is?"

"Probably cosying up to Matthew. I don't know," he said with a shrug. "You should leave. It's not safe for you here."

If he was going for the understatement of the year, Stephanie was ready to give him a prize there and then. "It's not safe for you either," she replied, then stepped toward the table. Even if she couldn't force Frank to go with her, she could still disable the pod – or at least destroy it.

"Leave that alone," protested Frank, stepping between her and the table.

"How do you open this thing?" she asked, pushing him aside. The question was not for Frank.

Before any instruction could rise from Gwyn, however, Frank forced himself between Stephanie and the pod once again. "You don't know what you're doing," he said.

"Because you do?" she retorted.

He looked at her, mouth agape. "Yes!" he said, as if he found her objection simply absurd.

It was clear to Stephanie that the boy was in over his head. "I don't think so."

She went to pick up the shovel from where she had left it. If Frank wasn't going to help her open the pod, she could always turn to other methods to secure the result she needed.

She wasn't going to have time for that, though.

As the door of the barn burst open, Stephanie reacted on instinct and threw the shovel at it before she even realised who the visitor was.

The door closed again just in time for the shovel to hit the woodwork and fall to the ground with a clang. When the door opened again, Damien was holding his gun, a silencer attached to its muzzle, ready to shoot. By then, however, Stephanie had already taken shelter behind one of the beams supporting the loft.

She knew it wasn't a great hiding place, but it offered her the best cover if Damien decided to shoot. She slid the knife from its sheath and readied herself for the fight ahead.

I can take him out for you.

It was far from ideal, yet still the best plan they had. Stephanie set her intention and trusted Gwyn to catch the drift of her thoughts.

"Mr Campbell, why don't you take the pod to the car. I'll take care of the rat in the barn," said Damien, his measured voice sending a shiver down Stephanie's spine. She knew he was relishing the moment.

While Gwyn made her way down her body, Stephanie heard Frank mumble something, then multiple steps moving around before the barn door closed and silence settled.

"Time to come out, Davis. It's just you and me now."

"I beg to differ," she responded, turning into view and drawing his attention away from Gwyn, who was already quickly scuttling towards him.

Something had gone amiss, though. Blind when disconnected from Stephanie, the Skaara had calculated a trajectory without accounting for movement. She had set her course on a straight line towards Damien's legs while he had kept approaching Stephanie's location.

When Stephanie lunged at him with her knife, it was already too late. He had spotted Gwyn on the ground.

Three muffled shots in rapid succession hit the ground around the Skaara, while Damien just about dodged the knife attack to his side.

There was no time to check what happened to her space sidekick. Stephanie took her chance to grab the gun and pin Damien's right arm against his side. She twisted the weapon out of his hands and heard the snap of a bone breaking as his finger got caught by the trigger.

Barely registering his painful cry, she kicked him in the stomach to create some distance yet failed to grab hold of the weapon. She watched it fall to the ground a few feet away.

Both aware of the firearm lying just out of reach, Damien and Stephanie paused, seizing each other up before the fight. He was clutching his hand, visibly in pain. She was clutching her knife, still unharmed.

Things were going her way.

She sliced the air with the knife, creating space for a body tackle just as he raised his arms to protect his face. She was about to push him to the ground and finish him when he managed to grab her leg, sending her flying backwards onto the floor instead.

The fall knocked the breath out of her. Before she could even start worrying about it, Damien's boot was raised over her head, ready to end the fight for good. Stephanie deflected the stomp just as it bore down on her, then hit back with a punch that only reached his thigh. The blow still bought her enough time to slip past him and throw a kick to his knee.

A better strike would have broken his leg, yet Damien barely stumbled sideways. Not what she had planned for, but she at least managed to get back on her feet.

Damien was waiting, holding his hand to his chest. Stephanie could see he was sweating, his breathing fast and shallow.

"Are you going to ask for a time-out?" she taunted him.

The idea was to make him lose his temper and, in doing so, his focus. If she could only get him to expose himself, maybe grab hold of his injured hand, she could finish him for good.

He wasn't paying attention to her words, though. His eyes were glazed over. Stephanie wondered if he could even see her.

She stepped aside, watching his movements, trying to find an opening. Before she could attack again, however, Damien feigned a low blow to her gut. As she went to block, she already knew her mistake in exposing her face to the blow that followed.

She staggered backwards, raising her arms to protect her head, while Damien placed a strong kick to her stomach instead, sending her gasping for breath, a sharp pain rising from her chest, as if new cracks were opening in her freshly healed ribs.

When she looked up again, the shovel she had left against the post was already coming fast towards her head. She managed to dodge one blow, only to leave her side open to the next.

It was all she could do to keep standing. Adrenaline was the only thing holding her up, and it was getting harder and harder to catch her breath.

Damien still kept on coming, holding the shovel as if it were a medieval sword, ready to thrust it into her stomach. She dodged and let him plunge past her.

Off balance, she couldn't do much more than push him on, until he turned on his heels and landed his next blow at the back of her head.

All she knew was that there was pain.

After that, only darkness.

- XV -

A cart house was not an impregnable fortress. Or at least that was what Lucy kept telling herself as she walked around looking for a way out.

She had spent minutes sitting on the floor, staring at the same spot of dust, trying to process what happened.

She had ruined everything. She had got in the way, got herself in trouble, and Avis Carmen was going to get their victory over the Skaara thanks to her.

For all the good planning that Davis had done around the fake beacon, Lucy had managed to give Damien Bennett the upper hand.

She should have stayed out of the way – to hell with getting involved and trying to do the right thing.

The right thing is a myth anyway, she thought, yet she found she didn't really believe that anymore. She closed her eyes as the hole in her stomach filled her eyes with tears.

She couldn't give up. She was going to get herself out of there and she was going to fix what she had broken.

Lucy leaned against the wall and exhaled loudly, releasing the tension tightening her shoulders.

She knew the door was securely bolted from the outside, and it had an old latch that she couldn't pick with a pin.

She moved a bench to reach the small window at the top of the back wall, but even on tiptoes she couldn't get close enough to open it.

As she landed back on the ground, she spotted a mallet leaning against the wall in the corner. Lucy turned to the door one more time. It was an old wooden frame with an old rusty lock. It couldn't have been hard to break.

The first blow hit the metal lock and bounced right back, the jolt reverberating up Lucy's shoulder. With a yelp, she let go of the handle, the mallet landing on the ground with a heavy thud.

"Okay, that could've gone better," she said to herself and to the empty room.

She slipped off her jacket, already feeling warmer from the exertion, then picked up the mallet again and scrutinised the lock. Running her fingers over the woodwork, she noticed the left side was slightly out of line, and the wood around it was somewhat more tender than the rest. That was the spot. She only had to swing right. "Here we go," she whispered again.

The second blow struck the lock, and Lucy heard the wood cracking, although she could see no signs of it breaking on the surface. It was going to take a while.

It was a very heavy mallet, and the sideways swing was exerting muscles Lucy wasn't sure she had ever used in her life. The strength in her arms and shoulders seemed to fade with each blow, forcing her to pause longer before the next swing. Even so, the lock was slowly budging under the pressure, and one more well-placed hit finally dislodged the metal casing.

"Just one more," she whispered as a way of self-encouragement.

She gathered the last of her strength, then let the mallet fall heavily on the lock with a pained grunt.

The whole door frame shook as the lock fell out of shape.

Lucy pressed her hand against the door, testing its resistance. It moved but didn't open.

"Oh, come on, you!" she protested, throwing herself against it, shoulder first. She almost stumbled to the ground when the door gave under her charge and let her out into the open.

For a moment, it felt as if the overcast Midlands sky was the best thing Lucy had seen in her entire life. She allowed herself a smile, yet there was no time to pause.

She ran towards the farmhouse as fast as her legs would take her, adrenaline rushing her on.

When she got there, everything seemed to be eerily in order. The barn door was closed, and Frank was standing by the SUV. Lucy could see the Skaara pod he had already loaded in the boot.

That's it, she thought. *That's how I'm going to fix it.*

Just then, Matthew walked out of the house to join him. He waved at her from a distance. She waved back, feigning a smile.

Damien and Victoria were nowhere to be seen. As much as she was sure they wouldn't try anything while Matthew and Frank were close by, their absence still unnerved her.

She allowed her breath to return to its natural rhythm before casually approaching the SUV.

"Hey boys, are we taking the pod for a ride?" she asked.

"Hey, you," reacted Matthew, wrapping an arm around her and kissing her on the forehead. "Where did you disappear to? I've been looking for you all morning."

"I thought I'd go for a walk. Everyone looked so busy. I didn't want to be in the way," she lied.

He looked at her with a frown. "Where's your jacket?" he asked.

Before she could reply, though, Frank had turned around and grabbed their attention. "It's good timing for you to come back.

We're moving out shortly," he said, gently closing the boot as if a bomb was rigged and ready to explode inside.

Lucy noticed him slipping what looked like a remote control into his back pocket. She made a mental note of it, just as the gentle pressure of Matthew's hand on her waist started guiding her away from her brother and towards the door of the SUV.

She couldn't know for sure, but it was likely Damien had adjusted Avis Carmen's landing plan to account for the fake beacon. That must have been the reason for the early departure.

As Matthew opened the back door of the car to let her in, she decidedly held back. "Why are we leaving? Didn't we just get here?"

Frank and Matthew exchanged a look before Frank said, "Change of schedule."

"What do you mean?" she insisted. "You're saying it as if the Skaara called and said they'll be here earlier."

Matthew shrugged. "All I know is that Damien had a chat with Uncle Jim, then came out saying we have to move. Maybe the Skaara did call after all."

Frank looked at Lucy as if he was trying to tell her something. "Damien's in the barn, if you'd rather ask him."

With a tug, she freed herself of Matthew's hold. "If Damien's too busy tinkering, that's no reason to keep the Skaara waiting, right?" she said. "If the word is go, I say we go."

She made her way towards the back of the car and brushed against Frank before grabbing his arm and pulling him in a hug.

"I'd say thank you, but... what are you doing?" he half-protested, stiffly enduring that display of affection.

She pulled away and casually patted him on the chest. "Just giving a hug to my favourite brother. It's an important day. I'm proud of you."

Lucy could see on her brother's face how unconvincing her performance had been. She had no time to worry about it, though, and instead used that moment of general confusion to slip along the side of the SUV towards the driver's door.

She paused for a moment to smile at the two men, utterly confounded by her behaviour. Not for long, though. Her hand soon found the door handle, and she slid into the car, locking herself inside.

Only then did Matthew and Frank realise what she was up to. However, the keys had been left in the ignition, so they had no way to stop her.

By the time she had turned on the engine and started towards the open countryside and the road ahead, the two had just started looking around the yard for another vehicle to use in pursuit.

Lucy barely cared about that, though. She had to take the pod away from there, maybe all the way to Herefordshire and the Duckworth estate, where the Lady of the Partridges was probably sitting on that uncomfortable sofa drinking lukewarm tea.

Wouldn't that be a fitting payback, she thought.

She pulled onto the road and pressed down the accelerator, reaching a dangerously high speed on the narrow country road. If she could get as far as the motorway, she could get away, get lost in the traffic, maybe even all the way to Herefordshire, or at least someplace where she could destroy the pod without injuring any Skaara or human.

Hope lasted only a handful of seconds, though. Soon enough, two Avis Carmen's SUVs appeared in the rearview mirror.

The road was narrow, and Lucy took confidence in it. She pressed on the gas. No matter how much they gained on her, they couldn't overtake or cut her off, though she knew things would change soon.

Then, she spotted a dirt road turning down to the left.

Change of plan, she thought, as she hit the brakes and turned – just as something hit the rear window.

When she glanced in the rearview mirror, the mark she saw on the rear window reminded her of a bullet shot.

Great, now they're shooting at me.

She wouldn't dare go any faster on that type of road, yet she knew her escape wouldn't last much longer.

Another bullet caught her side mirror.

In front of her, the road was taking her to an isolated storehouse, giving her no choice but to slow down. She had nowhere to go. They were going to kill her, no doubt about it, but she couldn't give up while the pod was still intact and operational.

There must be a way out, she thought, panic creeping up her chest.

Before she could figure out a new plan, however, one more bullet hit the rear mirror. It caught Lucy by surprise, and she jerked the steering wheel to the left enough to send the front wheel into the soft ground. She could have regained control, but when she pressed the accelerator again, her way forward had already been blocked.

Fine, she thought, *have it your way.*

She searched the dashboard for a button to open the boot. She pressed it just as she opened the door to get out. From her pocket, she extracted the remote control she had lifted from Frank and held it up, making it clearly visible to anyone around her.

She was sure they all knew what that meant.

Matthew popped out of the SUV closest to her, and Lucy

noticed that Frank had decided not to follow. Part of her was relieved, considering what she was about to do.

"Lucy, let's not do anything rash," said Matthew, as he carefully moved towards her, reaching out as if approaching an angry dog. "You don't even know what that remote is for. Just give it to me, please."

"Maybe I don't," she snapped back. "It sure looks like it's important, though, so I think I will keep it a bit longer."

At that point, as many as seven Avis Carmen agents had stepped out of their vehicles, ready to pounce on her. "Should we take her down?" one of them asked.

While Matthew considered the option, Lucy raised the remote higher. There were three buttons to push. She moved her thumb to find one of them.

A few moments earlier, she would have trusted her boyfriend to stop any attempt on her life. As they stared each other down across a few yards, she wasn't too sure about that anymore.

"No," he said finally. "Just give me a minute." He took a step closer to her, and everyone behind him did the same thing.

Lucy felt like a cornered animal. She had already been locked away once; she wasn't going to stand that treatment again.

She found the first button on the remote and pressed it.

Nothing happened.

Matthew didn't seem to have noticed. "Give me that remote, Lucy," he cautioned her. "We need that pod to handle the Skaara. You know that. And we need you too. Please, we're trying to save the planet, remember?"

She looked at the outstretched hand that Matthew was offering her, as if she was on the verge of a precipice and he was going to save her from falling – or as if he was about to give her the final push. "What if you start a war instead?" she asked in return.

Another step forward from Matthew, and the circle around Lucy grew ever smaller. "Nobody is going to start a war," he said. He had put on his condescending voice. He sounded so much like his father.

Lucy moved her thumb on the remote to find a second button. She pressed it. Nothing happened.

Her back against the car, Lucy leaned against the floor of the boot, the pod sitting next to her.

She was shaking. Pressing the first two buttons had felt like playing Russian Roulette and winning. The third one, however, was a sure shot. Frank had called it a lethal dose of benzodiazepines for the Skaara. She wondered how many humans it would take out.

"What if there is a better way?" she asked. Her gaze had dropped to the ground by Matthew's feet, her mind still alert to his movements. Her shoulder hunched in resignation at the gravity of the moment, yet she still held the remote high above her head for all to see.

The circle of men around her stepped a little bit closer.

Matthew's voice was so close he could have been whispering. "There isn't. Trust me."

Trust. She had tried that. It hadn't worked. "What if I don't?" She looked up at him for only a second, then added, "I'm sorry."

Her finger pressed the last of the buttons.

There was a whiff and a hissing sound, then a white cloud rose from the pod.

Everyone rushed to cover their faces, but Frank had done his job well. The cloud enveloped the world around them.

As Lucy fell into unconsciousness, there was a bitter smile on her face at knowing everyone else was also falling with her.

- XVI -

There was pain.

Pain was good. It meant she was still alive.

As Stephanie opened her eyes, though, she wondered if it wasn't a dream she was waking up to instead – or a nightmare.

In front of her, Victoria was swinging the shovel left and right while Damien tried his best to dodge the blows. In the effort to protect his broken hand, he didn't seem able to do much more than that.

The pain in Stephanie's chest was intense, and she was having a hard time breathing. Despite that, she had to help Victoria.

It was an immense effort to stand up without crying in pain, and she had to pause once she got on her feet, battling not to fall back to the ground. The barn post next to her held her up until her vision cleared again.

As Victoria swung the shovel again, Stephanie watched Damien dodge towards her. She didn't waste time planning her move and threw herself at him, her shoulder ramming straight into his injured hand. Both collapsed to the ground, both writhing in pain.

Stephanie managed to roll away and call out to Victoria, "Hit! Now!"

She had meant for her to knock him unconscious, a clean blow with the flat of the shovel. Instead, she watched the blade rip into Damien's chest and heard his ribs cracking at the impact.

His eyes lingered on his attacker with a confounded stare, as if he could hardly believe what was happening to him – and at whose hands.

With a raging grunt, Victoria pushed the shovel deep into his chest, leaning heavily on its blade as if she were trying to go through his body to dig his grave.

After all the pain Damien had caused her, Stephanie could hardly condemn her for that.

A moment later, Victoria stumbled back, leaving the shovel rooted in Damien's body. Her hands were shaking, and her face had turned ashen. "I think I'm going to be sick," she murmured, her hands holding her stomach.

"Take a deep breath," said Stephanie, still lying on the ground next to Damien's corpse.

There was no time for Victoria to breathe, though, as she turned to the side and threw up her breakfast. She then slumped to the ground, her hands shaking, her breath ragged. She wasn't going to be fine anytime soon, but Stephanie couldn't wait for her to pull herself together. "Victoria, we have to go. Do you think you can help me up?"

The woman nodded, then slowly stood up and moved to help Stephanie to her feet.

The sole effort to sit up had taken Stephanie's breath away in the most literal way. As she tried to stand up, the pain in her ribs was excruciating. She found herself wishing Gwyn were with her to dull the pain, then shook the thought away.

She let herself be walked outside, where the fresh air hit her face and hurt her lungs. She attempted a deep breath in. The pain was intense, but it didn't seem to be affecting the quality of her breathing – at least that was good news.

"Have you seen Gwyn?" she managed to ask.

Victoria shook her head. "She must have got away."

It made sense. With her eyes still closed, Stephanie let seconds pass. She didn't hear any sound from the inside, yet hoped the small Skaara was still hidden there.

"Victoria!"

It was a man's voice, yet Stephanie couldn't quite place it. Then she heard Victoria call out, "Campbell, what's going on?"

As she opened her eyes, Frank Campbell ended his run right in front of her, gasping for breath. "She took the pod," he managed. "Lucy took the SUV and drove off. Matthew followed her with some other agents. God knows what they're going to do! We've got to stop them."

Stephanie glanced at Victoria, silently seeking an explanation and wondering if she had misplaced her trust when sending Roxy to her.

"Don't look at me like that. I just about managed to keep the girl alive, but she's got a mind all of her own, you know that!"

Stephanie exhaled. Victoria was right: she couldn't blame her for Lucy's reckless actions. She turned to Frank. "What's in the pod?"

"Benzodiazepines," explained Frank. "A dose large enough to knock out the Skaara's fleet at the point of landing. If Lucy activates the pod, we have to hope she does it from a safe distance."

"Shit," murmured Stephanie, still trying to recover some strength in between pained breaths. "I should have told her. I swapped the beacons. There was no need for her to do that."

"She knew," said Frank. "And Damien knew as well. We were getting ready for plan B when she drove off."

Damien knew, and Lucy had taken matters into her own hands. Reckless, and dangerous. Yet part of Stephanie felt like praising Lucy's initiative. She only wished the girl hadn't put her life on the line for that. She pushed herself off the wall of the barn, struggling not to fall back against it right away. "Victoria, get your car. We're going after them."

Victoria hesitated. "Davis, are you sure you're okay to do this?"

"Go get your car, Victoria!"

The impetus she put in her words only brought Stephanie more pain, and a pang of nausea that threatened to send her swooning to the ground. She clenched her fists and tried to breathe through it. When she looked up again, Frank was the only one left with her.

"What happened in there?" he asked meekly.

"Payback," she replied, making it clear with her tone that she wasn't in the mood for interviews. Instead, she turned to poke her head through the barn door and looked inside. "Gwyn!" she called as loud as she could manage.

She heard an intake of breath behind her but ignored Frank's panic for the moment.

Her gaze surveyed the scene. Damien's body lay impaled on the ground while the makeshift laboratory remained untouched by the ordeal it had witnessed. She tried to pick out the shape of the Skaara. She knew Gwyn couldn't understand her words, but the sound of her voice and the vibrations through the air should have been recognisable enough.

A few long seconds passed, then the sound of tyres on the gravel announced Victoria's return. Stephanie exhaled. She thought she had seen the little scuttler slip away when Damien had shot at her. Everything had happened so quickly, though, she wondered if she had taken a hit after all.

As Victoria's quick steps approached, Stephanie found a hole widening in her core, joining up with the pain in her ribs. There had been a time when she would have killed the Skaara herself. How things had changed in just a few short months.

Stephanie pushed herself off the wall. She couldn't let grief overtake her. There was still the matter of Lucy. She had to try to save her.

You're in pain.

It was a new thought. A welcome interjection, and the one that introduced a new peace across her body. The pain left her just as relief washed over her.

"There you are," she murmured.

"Hold on, are you actually letting that thing on you?" protested Frank, noticing the Skaara clinging to Stephanie's waist.

"It's not as bad as it looks when you get used to it," she replied.

She started towards the car, just as Victoria called them back to action. "Hey, are we going or what?"

Stephanie took her place in the passenger seat while Frank settled in the back. "The SUVs took off in that direction, towards the road," he said, waving a finger straight in front of them.

"Are you sure you're trusting that one?" asked Victoria, loosely pointing at the backseat.

"It's his sister. I'm trusting that."

It took them moments to reach the road, where Victoria turned right without hesitation, following the skid marks left by the vehicles that had preceded minutes earlier and sending the Fiesta along the narrow country road.

"Any idea where Lucy might have gone, Frank?" asked

Stephanie, checking the countryside around them for anything that might look out of place.

"No," he replied. "She just locked herself inside and started the car. I didn't even think she'd know how to drive the SUV, but she figured it out quickly."

"Did she know what's in the pod?" asked Victoria.

"Yeah. She knows."

The silence stretched under the weight of that acknowledgement, until Stephanie ripped through it. "Stop! I see them!"

A few black vehicles sat at the bottom of a side road they had just passed, possibly half a mile away. She could have been wrong, and the idea caught her breath as soon as she uttered the words.

Victoria stopped the car with a screech of tyres. "Where?"

"A side road. We just passed it. Just drive back and turn left."

Stephanie was hoping with all her might for her instinct to be true.

Victoria reversed all the way to the side road, then turned in the direction Stephanie had pointed at.

As they approached the vehicles, Stephanie recognised three SUVs – the same ones she had spotted at the farm that morning.

"She activated it," said Frank, voicing what everyone else was already thinking.

Stephanie barely waited for the car to stop before opening the door and starting her search for Lucy amongst the bodies sprawled on the ground, only to find her lying right by the SUV, the pod open in its trunk.

There was a total of nine bodies spread on the ground around her. Matthew was the closest to Lucy.

"Get an ambulance!" she called back to Frank and Victoria as she knelt beside the girl. She pressed two fingers against her neck and waited to feel a heartbeat, murmuring softly, "Don't do this, please don't do this. Just stay with me. Please, Lucy, stay with me."

Then she felt it. It was feeble, but Stephanie was sure the heartbeat was there. She was about to turn to Victoria when she found her kneeling next to her, a first aid pack in her hands. "Epi-pen," she said, offering one to her.

Stephanie didn't need her to elaborate. She grabbed it and injected the adrenaline shot straight into Lucy's chest. Nothing seemed to happen.

"I think they're all still alive," shouted Frank somewhere behind her. Stephanie, however, wouldn't have cared either way.

"Did you call the ambulance?" she called back.

Victoria nodded next to her. "They're on their way, but it'll take time. We're in the middle of nowhere."

"We'll have to use your car, then."

"You want us to load all of them on the car?" asked Frank from the sidelines.

That wasn't what Stephanie meant. "They can wait for an ambulance, and you can wait with them if you like. Victoria and I will take your sister to the hospital." She then turned to Victoria. "You'll have to pick her up and bring her over to the car. I have too many bruised bones to do that myself."

"We can't leave the rest of them here like this," protested Victoria, albeit feebly, gesturing to the remaining crew on the ground.

They didn't matter, though, at least not to Stephanie. The ambulance could take care of the rest of Avis Carmen's agents, as well as Lady Partridge's favourite son.

Lucy wasn't going to wait that long.

***

It had been more than an hour before the doctor showed up to give them an update on Lucy's condition.

She was still asleep but solidly out of danger.

As Frank fell back on his chair with a sigh of relief, Victoria appeared round the corner with a cup of coffee. "Black, no sugar," she said as she handed it over to Stephanie, who took it with a thankful nod.

"They'll come for you," she said.

Victoria exhaled as she sat on one of the chairs opposite Stephanie. "I know."

Stephanie blew on her brew before taking a tentative sip. Gwyn was still wrapped around her waist, screening her from most of the pain. "You saved my life. Twice. I should be thanking you," she said.

Victoria shrugged, as if saving lives was her daily pastime. "We made a good team, while it lasted, didn't we?" she said.

"Yeah. We did." Stephanie stared pensively at her coffee for a moment. "I should get going. Look after her."

"Are you sure you don't want to stay?" asked Victoria, nodding towards the door of Lucy's room a few feet away. "I can go instead."

It was hard for Stephanie to admit how tempting that offer was. She shook her head lightly instead. "I'll be fine," she said with half a smile.

Victoria raised her eyebrows in surprise. "You seem very calm about it!" she remarked, applying her exclamation marks to a softer volume.

"I am," replied Stephanie simply. There was a chance Gwyn was keeping her nerves from bursting out of her skin, but she somehow doubted that. The hard part was done, and Lucy was going to be fine – just like everyone else caught by the benzodiazepine's cloud.

"Could you do me a favour?" Stephanie glanced at Lucy's room. "When her parents show up, make sure they know."

"What? That she saved the world from interplanetary war by overdosing on Xanax?"

Stephanie smiled in return. "Something like that."

It was hard to leave, knowing she wouldn't be back. Yet such was the nature of the life she had chosen.

As she walked down the hall to her date with the Skaara's spaceship, Stephanie left a part of herself behind – the part that wanted to stay with Lucy and make sure she recovered well; the part that wanted to meet her parents and tell them all the right and good things their daughter had done; the part that just wanted to go home, have a shower, and put all that behind her. Instead, she took with her the part that wanted to keep Lucy safe, and make sure she wouldn't have to take risks like that ever again – her and the rest of the world.

* * *

The rain had started tapping on the windshield a few minutes after Stephanie had parked the car on the side of the road.

The sky, still covered in clouds, had turned dark while they had been in the hospital, and the world around her looked like a vast pitch-black blanket.

By the time the lights of the Skaara spaceship broke through the clouds, the rain had turned into a gentle downpour.

It wasn't going to be a problem. Stephanie was going to stay in the car, while Gwyn was responsible for delivering the greeting message to the landing party. It was a practical way to welcome the visitors and, at the same time, demonstrate that their scout wasn't held hostage – at least not anymore.

Stephanie opened the car door just enough for Gwyn to slide out onto the muddy ground. As heavy drops fell on her sleeve from the roof of the car, she felt she should have said something momentous to mark the occasion. The Skaara, however, had already slithered away without a second thought.

She closed the door again, then turned off the engine. The windshield wipers halted mid-swipe as raindrops pooled across the glass.

She rested her head back and closed her eyes. She felt the pain in her chest growing stronger, so she took a long, slow, and deep breath, closing her eyes on the long exhale that followed.

When she opened her eyes again, she could barely see glimmers of light through the rain-covered windscreen.

She imagined Gwyn nested in the dirt, waiting.

She imagined the spaceship making contact with the ground.

That's it, she thought. *Three, two, one.*

Touchdown.

Acknowledgments

The past three years have been a challenge, and I couldn't be more grateful to all the amazing people who stood by me and supported me, through dark winters and broken bones - whether they found me at the writing table, on a football pitch, or in a long succession of dark Instagram reels.

Thank you all for accepting my weird, and gifting me your weird in return.

Of course, none of this would ever have happened without Jerry and Bonafide, who believed in this story even when it was mostly scattered thoughts and half-chapters. Thank you for still putting up with my ramblings.

Finally, to you, readers. Thank you for sticking around. This story is yours now.

Join Maddie Marzola's Reading Group

Click here to join **Maddie Marzola's Reading Group and newsletter** and get a free eBook download of The First Landing, or purchase the Skaara Series.

Head over to:

www.maddiemarzola.com

Please also consider leaving a review where you purchased this book. It's hugely appreciated.

Thank you!

About the Author

Maddie Marzola has been many things before becoming a writer - English tutor, science graduate, barista, football player, and ice cream vendor. Nowadays, she splits herself between an ordinary 9-to-5 clerical job and an extraordinary 5-to-9 writing life. Allowing for some sleep in between.

Science-Fiction is by far her favourite playground - a fascinating world of endless possibilities, a blank canvas on which to paint wild scenarios and impossible dreams. Not all of these make it into her books, but there's fun in trying.

The UK has been home for most of her adult life, and she found her writing family in Bristol.